In Her Own Time

Legacy Series, Book 2

PAULA KAY

ISBN: 0692434887
ISBN-13: 978-0692434888

DEDICATION

To Emily.
Thank you for your mentoring, support and friendship.
I look forward to the day that we can share a bottle of
Italian wine—preferably in Italy.

TABLE OF CONTENTS

CHAPTER 1

Lia walked across the kitchen with the last of the remaining food to be covered and put away for later. The wedding had been beautiful, the backyard something out of a magazine. She held back the tears that threatened to fall and surprised herself that they still came so easily whenever her thoughts turned to Arianna, which was often. Especially today, watching Gigi and Douglas take their vows in the garden that Arianna had loved so much. She would have been quite pleased with herself to see that her matchmaking had stuck. Lia giggled, thankful that the tears that had threatened had turned to more light-hearted memories of her daughter.

"What's so funny in here?" Blu grinned broadly as she entered the kitchen, crossing the floor to give Lia a quick hug and kiss on the cheek. "You really outdid yourself with dinner, Lia. It's as if we were transported back to Tuscany."

The two women locked eyes for a moment,

acknowledging what was left unsaid about Tuscany. The memories with Arianna there were some of the best that Lia had, and she suspected that Blu felt the same, even though Blu had a few more years of memories to draw from.

Lia hugged Blu back. "I was just thinking to myself how pleased Ari would have been about the wedding. And that reminded me of all the stories that Gigi and Douglas had told me about her attempts at getting the two of them together."

"It was quite a feat, if I do say so. Ari once told me, shortly after Douglas's first wife had passed, that she secretly knew he and Gigi belonged together. At the time, I discouraged her from saying anything. It was too soon. But she knew. She definitely had a sense when it came to matchmaking."

Lia stared intently at Blu for a moment. "Why do I get the feeling that you have something to tell me?" She grinned playfully at the young woman whom she'd grown very fond of over the last year.

"Mom, can I have some more ice cream?" Jemma bounded into the kitchen, interrupting the conversation momentarily.

"We'll talk more later." Blu winked at Lia. "And you, my darling daughter——" She patted the young girl playfully on the bottom. "——where are your manners?"

"Sorry, sorry." Jemma grinned at Lia. "Please, may I have a bit of ice cream, chef Lia?" she said in a very funny

British accent, causing the two women to burst out laughing.

As Lia got Jemma her ice cream and sent her on her way to eat at the table in the other room, Blu poured the two women a glass of wine. "Come, sit with me a minute."

Taking the wine out of her hand, Lia sat down at the breakfast table across from Blu, fully prepared to get all the scoop of what had been going on in her life since the big move to the beach house. "Tell me everything. Don't leave anything out." Lia grinned mischievously. She had spoken to Blu several times on the phone, but with the young designer's ambitious work schedule, it seemed she barely had a minute to catch Lia up on anything that was going on in her life.

Blu looked intently at Lia before she spoke, and Lia felt her chest tighten at the conversation that she knew was coming. "Why are you here, Lia?"

Lia felt herself bristle. "Of course I wouldn't miss the wedding."

"You know that's not what I mean."

Blu looked as if she was trying to be stern, but Lia knew that Blu, perhaps more than anyone, would understand her reluctance. Lia looked down as she gathered her words.

"Why haven't you made the move yet? It's been a year since—"

"I'm well aware of how long it's been. Trust me when

I say that I don't need any reminders about that day." She didn't mean for her words to sound so harsh, and as soon as they were out of her mouth, she was sorry for how she'd spoken to Blu.

Blu didn't brush away the tears that appeared suddenly in her eyes; Lia rushed over to her around the table, grabbing her in an embrace. "I'm sorry. You didn't say anything wrong. And I know your heart's in the right place."

The two women hugged for a moment, okay with the silence and each lost in her own thoughts about the day that they'd said goodbye to Arianna.

Finally Blu spoke. "There's not a day that goes by that I don't think about her. I still can't really believe that she's gone."

Lia nodded as Blu continued.

"I can only imagine how you must feel. I'm sorry. I shouldn't pry."

"It's okay. I didn't mean to react that way. I guess I've just been feeling a little edgy about everything. I don't want you to think that you can't talk to me about it. About anything. I'm sorry that I snapped," Lia said.

"Believe me, I totally understand about snapping these days." Blu laughed, which helped Lia to relax just a bit after their tense moment. "Honestly, Jemma is nearly driving me mad. I don't know what's gotten into her. She's behaving pretty well today, but the girl is getting to be a bit of a prima donna, if I do say so myself." Blu sighed in exasperation.

"Seriously, Blu, you need to nip that in the bud."

Lia didn't say out loud what she was thinking about the sudden change in the young girl's lifestyle. Basically she had gone from rags to riches, and Lia wondered if maybe Blu needed to start saying no to her daughter more often. But she would hold her tongue for now. It wasn't her place, and Blu wasn't asking her advice. Besides, what did Lia really know about being a mother? She couldn't keep herself from having the thought that was never completely out of her mind.

Choices. She hadn't been the best at making them. And there had been years of regret. Sometimes she wondered if she would ever be able to truly push that regret aside. Somehow, that voice in her head always won out; even after the amends, the good times; and the countless conversations with the only person that truly mattered when it came to her decisions. Even after Arianna's forgiveness.

"You okay, Lia? You seemed a million miles away just now," Blu said.

Lia sighed and looked up at Blu, who was gently touching her arm. "Sorry, what were you saying?"

"I was just agreeing with you that I needed to get to the bottom of the change in Jemma's behavior sooner rather than later."

Lia nodded.

"But can we talk about *you*, please? Now that we're

both in agreement that it's okay to talk freely?"

Lia could sense Blu's reluctance to continue the conversation, and she felt an obligation to give her the green light, putting her out of the misery that she'd had to endure earlier when Lia nearly bit her head off. She took a deep breath without even realizing it and nodded for Blu to continue. "Yes, go ahead."

"I'm just worried about you." The two women looked up as Gigi and Douglas entered the kitchen laughing at something that Douglas was whispering in Gigi's ear. "We all are, actually," Blu continued.

"We all are what?" said Douglas as he refilled the wine glass of his bride.

"You look so serious in here. Is everything okay?" said Gigi, and Lia saw the familiar crease of worry appear across her friend's forehead.

"Yes, never you mind. It's not the time for newlyweds to worry about anything. Blu and I were just catching up a bit," said Lia, hoping that Blu would drop it, but noticing the look pass between the two other women, already sensing that the conversation wasn't over.

"I was just about to ask Lia what her plans were. For the move and all," Blu said quickly, as if she had to jump in while she still had the nerve—and perhaps the backup of the happy couple, by the looks of things.

Lia sighed, knowing that there was no getting around the conversation. "Okay. So, why exactly is it that you all are worried about me?" She directed her question at all three of the people whom she'd grown to care for so much over the last year. They'd all been there at the end for Arianna, and they had continued to be there for one another in the time since. It was the closest thing to family that Lia had known since her own childhood, really, and she treasured their friendships a great deal.

Douglas fidgeted just a bit, looking to Gigi, and Lia couldn't help but notice that a whole conversation seemed to be taking place in that look. If she weren't so uncomfortable about being the topic of conversation, she'd make a joke about it. But now was not the time; Douglas was clearing his throat as if he had something important to say.

"Well, we were having a conversation earlier tonight amongst ourselves. Lia, you know we care about you. Actually, the thought of you leaving doesn't make us happy, and I know I can speak for Gigi in that regard."

Gigi laughed, and Lia knew without her saying it that the joke was partly about the meals that she loved to make for them on nearly a weekly basis. She smiled in spite of her discomfort as Douglas continued.

"It's just that it's been a year now since Ari—since Arianna passed away—"

Lia took a sharp breath in and squared her shoulders, surprised yet again at the stinging tears that she was desperately trying to hold back.

Gigi turned, giving Lia a big hug as Douglas continued.

"I know I—we certainly don't need to remind you how long it's been. We all think about her every day, Lia." He looked her in the eye, seemingly to ask for permission to continue, which Lia granted with a slow nod of her head.

"It's just that Ari wanted something for each of us. She was very clear about her wishes." Gigi crossed the short distance to stand beside Douglas, taking the hand that he offered her as he continued. "Honestly, I never would have believed that she would have been so right about Gigi and me. She seemed to know, long before this old dog did, how perfect this lovely lady would be for me." He brought their clasped hands up to his lips to gently kiss his bride's hand.

"Before Ari passed, she and I had many conversations about what she wanted for you, Lia," he said.

CHAPTER 2

Lia had always thought that Douglas was so genuine and kind. She had no reason to doubt his intentions or question what he was trying to say to her now—what they were all trying so gently to say to her. She let her shoulders slump as the tears came freely and she felt Blu reach for her hand across the table. Somehow she had found her way into this funny little group of people—her daughter's little family—another undeserved gift that Arianna had given to her. Lia smiled in spite of the tears because she knew how much her daughter would have loved that. It was one promise that Lia had kept so far.

"Do you not want the restaurant? Do you think that Thyme and Italy are too much for you right now?" Blu asked, and Lia could see the genuine question on her face.

Lia's thoughts turned again to a memory of Arianna, of the two of them in the sweet little restaurant that they'd discovered together in Tuscany. She couldn't help but smile as she remembered the little joke that they had shared about the name of the restaurant being Lia's favorite herb to cook with. She was so happy that Arianna had even known that much about her. It was crazy luck, really—the timing of it all. But Lia knew that it hadn't been luck at all.

It was destined that she would know her daughter before she died, and Lia also knew that Arianna had felt especially connected to the conversations that they'd shared together during their time in Tuscany. She had chosen Thyme for her because she knew what it would mean to Lia. *Why couldn't she just accept it?*

Lia took a deep breath as she contemplated that question in her head, and the question that Blu had asked her. *Could* she make a life for herself in Italy? And the restaurant—Thyme was everything that she'd ever dreamed of. She felt it deep inside; and suddenly, without even really thinking about it, she was nodding her head in response to Blu, who was asking her for a second time if she wanted to go to Italy.

"Yes, I do want it." She looked up at her friends. "I want it so badly. For myself, but also for Ari. I still have to pinch myself to believe everything that she's done for me." She cleared her throat to keep herself from letting out a sob as she continued.

"I don't deserve any of it. I would give it all back and more to have her back with me. To know her for more than the short time I knew her. It was all way too soon, and I guess I—I can't help but feel guilty for taking it." She couldn't keep the tears from falling again but she could sense something shifting inside her. It felt more like a release of sorts than the tears that had been burdening her almost daily since Arianna's death.

Gigi leaned in once again to give Lia a big hug. "We all would rather have Ari than the things she's left us. But she knew that, Lia." She looked at Lia as if for permission, before continuing.

"And I say this, not to hurt you, because I know that you made the best decisions you knew how to make when you gave Ari up." Lia nodded for Gigi to continue. "I've known Ari since she was a little baby, and that girl had everything money could buy. I had seen her go through so many phases, and a lot of them weren't pretty. You would have thought she was a spoiled brat when she was a teen-ager, and she was."

Douglas looked at Gigi, and Lia thought maybe he was wondering, as she was, where Gigi was going with her speech.

The look Douglas was giving her did not go unnoticed by Gigi as she continued. "I tell you this because of all the things that I've seen Arianna do and have during her lifetime, I've never seen her as happy as those final months that she spent with you, Lia." Gigi reached over to the table to get a napkin to wipe the tears that were flowing freely now.

"She had truly grown to love you and considered herself to be your daughter. She thought so carefully and prepared so well before she died. Douglas knows this more than anyone. During the final months of her life, she became the woman that she was always meant to be, and I think it gave her great joy to think of our needs." Gigi looked around the table, and it was then that Lia noticed that Jemma had crawled up onto Blu's lap, taking in the conversation with the wide eyes of a child who knew that she was witnessing an adult conversation.

"She knew us well and she knew the things that would make us happy, not instead of having her here, but in spite of her having to leave us."

Douglas and Blu nodded in agreement, and Lia noticed Blu hugging Jemma to her as if to solidify that the little girl was a part of the great legacy left by their dear friend that had loved them all so greatly.

Lia looked around her and smiled widely. "So it's settled, then. I hear you all loud and clear. I will make my pilgrimage to Italy—under one condition."

Her friends waited for her to continue, but not before Jemma piped up from the table.

"What is it, Lia?" she asked with her eyes wide.

The adults laughed as Lia continued. "I want you all to promise me a big reunion—I'll throw a party, in fact." She turned to Douglas and Gigi. "When did you say that you're going to Italy for your honeymoon?" She'd be excited at the prospect of seeing her friends very soon after her move.

"Now that is an excellent idea, and one that I think could very likely happen," Douglas said with a wide grin as he turned to Gigi, waiting for a reminder on the dates.

"In fact, we leave six weeks from today," Gigi called out from across the room, where she'd gone to check her calendar.

"Blu, do you think you can clear your schedule?" Lia gestured to Jemma. "And I don't suppose this one can get some time off from school?" Lia winked at Jemma.

"Oh, can we go, Mom? Can we? I want to go back to Italy again." Jemma seemed beside herself with excitement, while waiting to hear Blu's response.

"Oh, I think we can arrange something." Blu winked at Lia.

"Good, it's settled then." Lia walked across the room to retrieve the bottle of wine that Douglas had opened. "Now, how about a toast to the happily married couple?"

"I'll drink to that," said Gigi, reaching out her glass for a refill as Douglas leaned over to kiss her on the lips.

"To my bride," said Douglas as everyone raised their glasses in a final round of toasts.

"And to Ari," Gigi said, "for without her, who knows if this handsome man ever would have taken me seriously."

The group laughed as they raised their glasses again in a toast to Arianna.

PAULA KAY

CHAPTER 3

Lia pulled her bathrobe tight as she walked to answer the door of her apartment. She wasn't expecting someone this early in the morning; it was unusual, to say the least.

She peered out the peephole, grinning as she opened the door for Gigi, who was carrying a stack of moving boxes.

"I come bearing gifts."

Lia took the boxes from Gigi's one hand as Gigi reached for the coffee carrier in her other. "Including your favorite double espresso from down the street."

"Nice. I'll take it, thanks. Have a seat."

"Sorry to barge in unannounced," said Gigi, but Lia smiled to herself as she thought that Gigi looked anything but sorry.

"I thought I'd come by to help you do some packing." Gigi glanced at Lia. "And I guess I didn't want to give you the chance to say no. You know, I figured maybe you could use some moral support."

"Well, that, my friend, could be very true." Lia thought to herself that Gigi didn't even know the half of what she'd been feeling since the wedding and the big conversation that had taken place between her and her friends. She'd gone back and forth in her own head about making the decision to really leave. It seemed an impossible task to actually get from where she was now to her new home in Italy. But Lia had a sneaky suspicion that her friends were going to hold her to the promise that she'd made just a few days earlier. She looked at Gigi sitting across from her and sighed. Gigi's being here right now was proof of that fact.

"Well then. Where shall we start?" Gigi said, not missing a beat and barely taking the time to sip her coffee.

Lia laughed. "Well now, aren't you just raring to go?" She got up from the sofa where they were sitting. "Let me just go slip some jeans on and I'll be right with you. I guess we may as well start in the kitchen."

Gigi got up too. "While you're getting dressed, I'm going to go get something else from my car."

"More boxes?" Lia called from her bedroom.

"Nope. It's something of Ari's."

Just like that, Lia felt as if she'd been punched in the gut. She sat down heavily on the bed and tried to take a deep breath to calm herself and to stop the tears that threatened to fall. Just when she'd thought that she couldn't possibly shed another tear, they came so easily.

She'd never known grief like the grief she'd felt since Arianna's death. One might have thought it would be easier on a mother that hadn't raised her own child, but that wasn't the reality that Lia found herself in. She grieved for the woman that she had come to know as her daughter, but she also grieved for all of the years and mistakes that she had made prior to their meeting. Her grief was an onion that needed to be peeled back every day. Layer upon layer of shame, guilt, and anguish to discover, and it didn't really seem to be getting any easier.

Lia heard Gigi come back in, and she struggled to compose herself. She threw on jeans and a sweatshirt and crossed the hall to the bathroom, where she quickly splashed some cold water on her face. "I'll be right out," she called.

"It's okay. Take your time. I don't need to be anywhere today if you don't," said Gigi.

Lia composed herself, and then met Gigi in the kitchen; she was already assembling some packing boxes.

"Do you want to pull out the things that you don't think you'll be needing right now?" said Gigi.

"Asking a chef that is like asking her to choose among her babies." Lia laughed. "I'm sure there are some things I can put away. Gigi, I don't have a set date yet, you know."

Gigi gave her a quick look, which Lia decided to let pass for the moment as they packed a few boxes in easy silence.

Lia stopped her packing suddenly to face Gigi. "So what's in the box?" She recognized it as the one that Arianna had so carefully picked out while they were at the market in Florence together. Even the quick memory felt sharp and painful.

Gigi took her by the hand and guided her back to the sofa where she had placed the box. They sat on either side and Gigi carefully removed the leather lid, exposing the treasures that lay inside, on top of the deep red velvet lining. At a glance, Lia could see how much of Arianna was in that box.

"These are the things that Ari wanted her daughter to have." The two women looked at one another as Gigi continued. "When the time is right."

Lia nodded in silent acknowledgement about the contents of the box. Arianna had mentioned it to her also—before she died. Lia struggled to hold back the tears that threatened once again. She hadn't really known her daughter for long at all, but so many memories were there, all of them bittersweet. Lia sighed and moved the contents of the box just enough to get an idea of the items inside. She was fully aware that there had been a second urn of Arianna's ashes. One that matched the one in Lia's keeping, one of the pair that Arianna had picked out herself with Douglas's help. And here it was suddenly in front of her. In the box, so carefully packed for the daughter that Arianna would never know. The daughter that would never know how amazing her mother had been.

It wasn't over for Lia when it came to making amends with Arianna. It was almost an unbelievable twist of fate that Arianna, too, had been faced with similar choices in her own young life, though unwillingly; at the pressure from parents, irrevocable decisions were made. Decisions that would separate mothers and daughters. Lia would try to right the wrong once again. To the best of her ability, she hoped to one day meet her granddaughter, and she would gladly pass on the memories and wishes of her mother to her.

She turned to Gigi now with the obvious question that loomed unsaid between them. "Has Douglas had any luck finding the parents?"

"We were going to tell you the latest the other night, at the wedding. But then—well, with everything that happened, it didn't seem like the right time."

Lia sensed some bad news coming and instinctively sighed. "Go on."

"The private detective that he hired did locate the adoptive parents."

Lia sat up straight, feeling both excited and terrified at the prospect of learning about her granddaughter. The only thing that she knew up until now was that she would be about seven years old. "Where are they living?" she asked Gigi.

"Douglas couldn't really talk about specifics, but I do know that they are living in Connecticut."

Lia nodded for Gigi to continue.

"So the parents did speak to Douglas after a few phone calls. I'm sure that they were taken aback, because the adoption had been closed and they were pretty much assured that this wouldn't happen."

"I can only imagine how surprised they must have been." Lia couldn't help but contrast this to how Arianna must have felt the first time that Lia had phoned her. She later told her about the huge mixture of emotions and how difficult it had been to process everything. But Lia also now knew the other circumstances that Arianna had been dealing with. The things she wouldn't find out until much later that had greatly influenced the time that they'd been able to have together.

Gigi went on. "So after many attempts, he finally assured them that he just wanted to speak with them about their daughter's birth mom. He told them that she had passed away, but that he had promised her that he'd do his best to one day find the little girl that she'd given birth to."

"As you can imagine, I'm sure the news of Arianna's death was not only shocking but reassuring in a way. Just in the sense that there wasn't a biological mother out there threatening to be emotionally involved in the life of the daughter that they'd raised. Well, that's how I would imagine feeling myself, anyways."

Lia nodded in agreement. She had often wondered about this herself over the years, and it was one reason that she hadn't tried to contact Arianna earlier. She might not had ever gotten the courage up, if she was being honest with herself. But then the accident happened and something inside of Lia felt that losing her adoptive parents might just be too much for the daughter she, herself, had never known. Making that initial phone call to Arianna had been the biggest risk and the biggest reward that Lia had ever known, and she would always be so grateful for that time that they'd had together.

She only wished now that Arianna would have had the same opportunity with her own daughter. It was a terrible twist of fate, really. Unfair to lose your life so young; Lia still couldn't quite get over the shock of it all.

"So what did they say to Douglas? Did he tell them about the trust?" said Lia.

"Yes, they took some time to think about everything and when they called Douglas back a few days ago, they said that they'd decided to wait. Their daughter did know that she was adopted. They haven't hidden that from her, and she's too young to ask many questions, really. Basically, they said that they wouldn't be sharing anything with her until she was old enough to start asking questions. Once she's eighteen, if it becomes important to her, they would put her in touch with Douglas."

"But the trust? Did Douglas tell them about the money?"

"He did, yes. He told them that there was a lot of money set aside for their daughter and that Arianna's wishes were that she have it as soon as possible. That the will would make her them the guardian of the trust before she turned eighteen."

"And they didn't want to do that?" Lia asked, truly feeling a bit shocked.

"You know, Douglas said that the parents didn't seem very bothered about the money. They didn't ask how much it was, and Douglas didn't volunteer it once he knew how adamant they were with their decision. His gut feeling is that the girl will eventually start asking questions, and at that time the money will be one of many surprises to her. And if that never happens, once she turns eighteen, the parents will speak to her about the money and then the decision will be hers."

"So in other words, it's going to be a long time before I get to meet my granddaughter?" Lia said more to herself than to Gigi, really.

"Yes, I suspect that's true." Gigi gave Lia a quick squeeze. "And in the meantime, you are the keeper of the treasures. Shall we look at them together?"

Lia shook her head. "No, I don't think so. Not right now." She put the lid back on the box. "I'll save that for another time if you don't mind."

Gigi nodded her understanding as she pulled something out of the handbag beside her. "So there's another reason for me turning up unannounced with the packing boxes so early this morning." She handed Lia a rectangular envelope.

"What's this?" Lia had the feeling that she might be surprised by the contents of the envelope, and not exactly in a good way.

"It's your plane ticket. To Florence."

Lia narrowed her eyes and tried to calm herself as Gigi continued.

"Douglas bought it for you yesterday, and the flight leaves one week from tomorrow."

"Gigi, one week? Seriously? That's not nearly enough time for me to be ready." Lia didn't try to hide the annoyance that she was feeling now.

Gigi laughed, and Lia suspected that she'd known the reaction that she would get from her.

"It is actually changeable. You can change the date if you need to. So relax." She reached over to give Lia another hug. "But after our conversation the other night, we just thought maybe getting this, putting it in your hand, might actually help you to take the step. And it's why I'm here with the boxes to let you know that I've cleared my schedule for the next week to help you with whatever you need. And Lia—"

Lia, still a bit shocked, nodded for Gigi to continue.

"We all really want this for you. Ari wanted this for you. And it's going to be amazing."

Lia sat back on the sofa, staring at the ticket in her hand. She took a deep breath and let the quick flood of memories rush over her again. Arianna did want this for her. She had been so clear as they said their goodbyes to one another, and Lia remembered her huge smile as she delivered the news that she'd bought Thyme for her. She wanted Lia to make new memories there, in the restaurant and in Tuscany, the place that they'd grown so fond of while they were together.

Lia rose to her feet with what seemed like a new resolve. "Okay then. I guess we have a lot of work to do around here." She laughed, knowing that Gigi was probably feeling relieved to be off the hook regarding all the news that she'd already delivered in one short morning.

Gigi rose too and gave Lia a big hug before they made their way back to the kitchen. "So I guess we can start packing everything in this kitchen after all." She winked and Lia laughed, already pulling her favorite items out of the cupboards.

CHAPTER 4

Lia could hardly believe how fast the last few days had gone. She'd been packing and getting things done bit by bit, but now it was really getting to be crunch time. She laid her paper and pencil on the dining room table, before walking into the kitchen to pour herself a glass of wine. Out of habit, she poured from the bottle of Chianti, a wine she'd only really begun drinking after she met Arianna. It had been her daughter's favorite, and like many things that Lia did these days it only served to remind her of what she'd lost.

She had to laugh as she crossed the room to turn on the CD that she knew was ready to go. It was *La Bohème*, Arianna's favorite opera. Lia still found it hard to believe that her daughter had loved opera so much; it had been such a foreign thing to Lia before Arianna had introduced her to that world. She admitted to herself, that it still wasn't her favorite, but she did find it relaxing, and of course it mostly served to bring memories of their time together which Lia was not yet ready to let go of.

Lia settled herself at the table and looked at her list.

She was actually feeling a bit surprised at the things that were left. She only had to pack up the few things left in the kitchen, and her clothes that were going with her, in the bedroom. Everything else was packed away in boxes, tucked away in the storage space that she'd rented. Douglas would have everything shipped once she was settled and ready for it. *Assuming that she'd stay in Italy.* God, where had that thought come from? Of course she was going to stay. What else would she do, anyways?

She suddenly remembered that she did need to call the agency. They'd been so good about working with her and keeping her file up-to-date after Arianna's death. Occasionally they would call her because a good job had come up.

The best ones, that Lia had a hard time turning down, were the ones that only needed a chef, someone to handle all of the cooking and grocery shopping for the household. Lia knew from a lot of experience that the families without housekeepers, or worse yet, the ones with children but that didn't have nannies, could be a nightmare to work for.

The jobs all started out the same. There was a lot of cooking and everything that Lia loved, but soon other things would sneak into the job requirements. Helping to ready the whole house for guests when the regular housekeeper called in sick, watching the toddler while the mom ran downtown for a few "quick" errands. These were the jobs that made her want to rethink her chosen career path.

None of this really mattered now, of course. And even this last year when it would come up in conversation with Gigi and Douglas, they gently reminded her that she didn't need to work anymore. Arianna had left her plenty of money to retire or do whatever she wanted. When they were alone, though, Gigi did tell her that she could understand it. It was something the two women had in common, and some days Gigi also found it difficult to not be working. So she was a silent supporter of the fact that Lia still had her file on hand at the agency. Lia didn't really want to go back to that kind of job either, but on the roughest days, the days when she felt so emotionally drained that she could hardly get out of bed, she wondered if the work might be good for her—give her a purpose of sorts.

But she had the restaurant and a new life waiting for her in Italy now—hardly anything to complain about. She'd call the agency in the morning to tell them that they could delete her file for good.

Lia added the item to the list, and her thoughts turned to what the past year had been like. Other than Gigi and Douglas, she really didn't have anyone else in her life to see or say goodbye to. She didn't know whether to feel relieved or sad about that fact, if she was being honest with herself. She'd always had at least a small close-knit group of girlfriends before moving to the Bay Area, but when she'd made that move her only purpose had been to spend time with Arianna. She had cared little back then about making new friends; and since Arianna had passed, it was really the last thing that she'd thought about. She'd had Gigi and Douglas in her life, which had been a godsend. And of course Blu and Jemma, before they'd moved down to San Diego. That little group of people— Arianna's little extended family—had become everything to Lia.

Gigi had gently tried to talk to her about her social life on different occasions, saying that maybe it would be good for Lia to get out and meet some people. She hadn't said as much to her, but Lia guessed that Gigi worried about her. The truth was that some days Lia didn't even really want to get out of bed. She'd toyed with the idea of seeing a therapist, but that even seemed a path that she wasn't ready to go down.

She'd taken to going to the Catholic church by her house. She wasn't really a religious person, even though her parents raised her in the church. But she found a certain sense of calm and peace there on particularly darker days. On occasion, she would open up to one of the priests there and his words always made her feel better, reminding her of God's ways and a bigger purpose for everything. Lia didn't really know how much of that she believed, but it seemed to make her feel better, nonetheless. She made another note on her list to visit the church one last time before she left.

Lia took a last sip of her wine and, satisfied with her

list, walked into her bedroom to get the suitcase down from her closet. It was time to pack up the last of her clothes and the things that would be going with her in just a few days.

She slid her closet door open wide and took a deep breath as she reached for the box on the shelf overhead. Laying the wrapped object aside on her bed, she unfolded the black jacket and held it up to her face, taking in a deep breath. If she closed her eyes, she could imagine that Arianna was in the room with her. Or that the two of them were back in Florence, getting ready for the nice dinner that Arianna had organized for them.

When Gigi had invited Lia and Blu over to help her with Arianna's closet, they'd selected one item each to keep. Gigi had suggested that they should take whatever they wanted, but they all had agreed that the clothing should go to a local charity. There was one that helped women to get back on their feet with interviews and new jobs, and Arianna's vast wardrobe was a great donation for the organization. They knew how pleased it would have made her.

Lia had chosen the jacket that Arianna had worn in Florence during one of their first dinners out. She didn't tell the other women this, but one of the main reasons for her selection was the fact that Arianna's perfume had been so strong on the jacket. Lia could still smell her daughter whenever she took the item out of her closet, although the scent was so much less now than it had been a year ago. But she wasn't ready to leave the jacket behind. It was coming to Italy with her along with the urn of Arianna's ashes.

Before Lia could stop to wonder if it was strange to be taking the urn in her suitcase—or even worse, against some kind of law—she wrapped it up tight in another layer of tissue paper, placed it in a smaller box, and tucked it in the corner of her suitcase, among the clothing that had already been packed there. She wasn't willing to have it shipped with the rest of her boxes, so among her clothing was the only logical choice that she could see.

Lia sighed and continued to pack up the rest of her clothes. She smiled for a moment when she came to the black dress that Blu had made for her. It was a gorgeous piece from her new line, black with her signature dash of bright blue in the inside lining. When Blu had given it to her last week, she had joked about it being perfect for a night out with a handsome Italian man in Lia's near future. Lia had laughed and gone along with the joke, responding that she doubted that would happen; but in any case, she should have a nice dress, more suitable than her own clothes—which weren't anything out of a fashion magazine, for sure.

She carefully placed the dress inside the garment bag it had come in, noting Blu's cool label inside. She made a mental note to call Blu, because she'd been wanting to talk to her more specifically about her new business. It was wonderful to see that Blu finally had the time to focus on her clothing, and Lia knew that it was just a matter of time before the young designer's career really took off.

Lia finished up the last of her packing and took a look around her empty apartment. Maybe she'd pull just a few items back out of the kitchen boxes she'd left until the last minute; that way that she could make one last little Italian feast for herself before she added her apron to the suitcase.

PAULA KAY

CHAPTER 5

Lia lay her head back against the leather seat in the car that Douglas had sent for her. It was hard to believe that the last of her boxes were packed up and in storage and that she'd handed the keys over to her landlord just moments ago. She looked out the window as the car pulled away from the modest apartment complex where she'd been living for the last year or so. Gigi and Douglas and even Blu had tried to convince her to move somewhere a bit nicer, and closer to them in Marin. God knew that she had the money now, and Arianna would have loved to have seen her in a more luxurious place. But Lia hadn't been ready for that. It felt weird—just leaping into another standard of living when she had learned to survive on the money she was making as a housekeeper and chef. It had been a struggle for sure, but one that she hadn't really minded for the most part.

Embracing the restaurant and the move to Italy that Arianna had made possible for her was one thing; learning to live with the kind of wealth that her daughter had left her was quite another thing altogether. So far, she didn't think she was really doing such a good job of it.

Her thoughts turned to Blu, because in some ways they were so much alike. The two women had grown close over the past year, but Lia felt that there were still so many things that Blu kept to herself. She was really a very private person, and Lia sensed a lot of struggle and heartache in her past. She never pried, but lately their conversations had been a bit more personal when it came to Blu's life, so she felt that the time was coming. She remembered the night of the wedding, before the conversation had turned to her. It seemed that Blu had been about to share something important with her. She'd have to remember to bring that up with her when they spoke.

She sighed as she suddenly realized that she wouldn't be seeing Blu and Jemma until their arrival in Tuscany in a few months. Perhaps a good phone conversation would have to do until then.

The car ride to Sausalito went quickly, and Lia took in the view as they crossed the bridge. She never tired of it, and this crossing made her think of Arianna once again, as it did every time she made the trip.

Minutes later the driver was helping her collect her large suitcases as she stood on the doorstep of Gigi and Douglas's home for what she knew would be the last time in a long while. It was funny how much this house had become a second home to her. First, while she spent the time there with Arianna, and since then, all the many dinners and special occasions celebrated there with Gigi and Douglas, who had really become her very best friends.

She was jolted out of her thoughts by a high-pitched squeal of laughter and Jemma flinging herself at her in delight.

"Surprise." Jemma giggled, holding on tight to Lia's waist to give her the kind of big squeeze that only a seven-year-old could give.

"Jemma, be careful. You're gonna knock poor Lia over." Blu laughed, appearing in the doorway to give her friend a big hug. "Are you surprised?"

Lia was laughing and crying at the same time. "Yes, I'm surprised, and so delighted that you two are here. Why didn't you tell me that you were coming?"

"We wanted to surprise you." Jemma grinned. "And it worked."

"Yes, it did indeed." Lia knelt down to give the little girl a big kiss on the cheek. "You have just made my day, young lady."

"Great," Jemma screamed and ran off towards the kitchen.

"Jemma, don't bother the chef now. Go play outside, okay?" Blu called out and then shrugged when she didn't get a response. "She's been bothering them in the kitchen to make her favorite grilled cheese sandwiches for dinner."

The two women laughed and Lia reached out to

embrace Blu. "Thank you so much for being here. It really means a lot to me."

"Are you kidding? We had to come see you off on your adventure." Blu's tone suddenly turned more serious. "I'm really proud of you, Lia. I know this is a big step for you, and it's gonna be great. I can feel it."

"I hope you're right, my friend," Lia replied with just a hint of worry in her voice. "Now where are Gigi and Douglas hiding?"

"Oh, I'm sure Douglas will be around soon with the wine. They're getting the table ready for dinner. We all thought it would be a nice idea to eat outside in the garden. It's such a nice night."

"That sounds absolutely perfect to me. Let's go see about that drink. I kinda feel that I could use one." Lia laughed and the two women headed to the kitchen.

Before they could make it inside the doorway, Douglas met them with a bottle of wine and glasses. "Sorry, I was just outside helping Gigi and a little bird flitted—well, more like rocketed by—" Douglas laughed. "—to let us know of your arrival. Come, let's get you two situated in the living room for a drink before dinner. We have a few minutes before it will be ready. I think it will be worth the wait, as the young chef comes highly recommended by one of our dear friends."

Lia and Blu took the wine that Douglas handed to them and sunk into the comfortable sofa.

"Won't you sit and have a drink with us?" Lia said to

Douglas, who was already halfway across the room.

He laughed. "Sorry, I don't mean to be rude. I want to get back to Gigi and her table. You know that woman. No matter what I say, she's always looking after everything. The chef's team are perfectly capable of setting the table, but she wants it to be just so."

Lia laughed. "Oh, I understand. Go on. We'll chat later at dinner."

Lia turned her attention back to Blu on the sofa beside her. "So, speaking of young good-looking chefs—"

"He didn't say anything about the chef being good-looking." Blu laughed.

Lia laughed too but didn't want to miss the moment to find out a bit more about what was going on with Blu. "How are things with you and your chef? What's his name again?"

She thought that Blu was blushing slightly, but she really didn't want to let her off the hook.

"His name is Chase and, you know, things are fine. There's nothing serious going on between us but yes, we've been out a few times. He's a nice distraction from all the craziness that has become my life, and Jemma seems to like him, so that's a good thing."

"*That* is a very good thing," Lia said. "Although honestly, is there anyone that little girl doesn't take to?"

"Good point." Blu laughed. "She is very charismatic and definitely not afraid to meet new people, which is actually something that drives me crazy."

Lia thought she saw something flicker in Blu's eyes. It was one of the moments she'd seen before, any time that the two women seemed to hit on a topic of a personal nature involving Blu and Jemma. And true to form, Blu was up and moving, eager to move on from the conversation.

"Let's go find Gigi and see if we can help with anything. Well, I'll help. You should sit and enjoy the night as the guest of honor." Blu smiled widely and Lia made a mental note to come back to the topic of Chase and the craziness that Blu had mentioned. The girl really didn't like to talk about herself at all.

CHAPTER 6

Lia followed Blu to the garden, noticing the delicious smells coming from the kitchen. "Wow, something smells divine," she said to Gigi as she looked up from the flowers that she was arranging. Lia crossed the grass to give the woman a big hug. "As do you, lovely. And everything looks so beautiful, including yourself, as usual."

Gigi grinned, hugging her back. "Nothing but the best for you on this special night. I'm so happy to have you here, and thrilled that you'll all be spending the night. It's always nice when this big home has lots of company." She turned to wink at Douglas, who was watching her from a chair close by. "Isn't that right, darling?"

"It is indeed," Douglas said. "Love and laughter within these walls. That's the goal." He'd come up behind Gigi as he spoke, giving her a playful pat on the behind.

Gigi, looking mortified, swatted his hand away. But then she laughed as she gave him a quick kiss on the lips. "Oh, you. Watch yourself."

Lia and Blu laughed, and Jemma looked up from where she was playing nearby. "Grown-ups. Who can understand them?" she said, appearing to be talking to herself—which made everyone laugh even harder.

"Dinner is about to be served, if you could take your seats, please."

The young chef—who was in fact very good-looking, Lia noticed—appeared with a small wait staff right behind him.

Lia caught Blu's attention and mouthed the word "cute". The two laughed as they all took their seats, admiring the fancy plates of food put before them.

"What a lovely dinner. Thank you so much for doing this," Lia said to Gigi and Douglas.

"It's our pleasure. You've served us so many wonderful meals over the span of the last year, it's a delight to be able to treat you to one. I only wish that I could have made it myself, but we all know how that would go." Gigi laughed and Douglas chimed in right after.

"Oh, darling, your scones and Italian coffee are to die for. Keep on making me those for breakfast and everything is okay in my world." Douglas leaned over to kiss his new bride on the cheek.

Lia couldn't help but grin as she saw the two together. What a journey they'd been on; it was wonderful to see them so in love and happy, right here in Arianna's garden and the home that she'd loved.

Gigi looked pointedly at Blu. "Now speaking of good-looking young chefs…" She winked, and Blu nearly choked on the wine she was sipping.

Lia laughed. "Great minds think alike. I was just asking her about Chase a few minutes ago."

"I like Chase really a lot," Jemma chimed in. "He builds sand castles with me and makes me the very best grilled cheese sandwiches." She stopped to take a bite of the sandwich on the plate in front of her. "Better than these." She wrinkled her nose and pushed the plate to the side a little bit.

"Jemma Lynne." Blu glanced toward the kitchen as she gave the little girl a stern look. "That is very impolite. And I think you know better than that."

Jemma looked down at her plate and picked up her sandwich again. "Sorry, Mom." She looked over at Lia and whispered, "But it's true."

"Jemma." Blu raised her voice a tad.

"Well, it is," Jemma said a bit defiantly.

"Just eat your dinner." Blu looked at the others and gestured towards the sky as if calling on heaven. "That girl."

"Mom, it's not nice to talk about me when I'm right here," Jemma piped up in an exaggerated tone.

"Okay, that's enough now." Blu turned towards Lia. "As you were saying?"

"Oh, well, we were just talking about your love life, weren't we?"

All of the adults burst out laughing, even Blu, who was blushing at this point, trying to recover; Lia guessed she was trying to think of a way to change the topic of conversation, which was going nowhere fast.

"Well, it is worth saying—that you and Chase were also one of Arianna's matchmaking projects. Isn't that right, Blu?" said Gigi. "Actually, I remember when she was arranging the chef for that first weekend she took you to the beach house." She winked at Blu. "She really did think that the two of you would hit it off."

"And I guess she was right," Lia said.

"Well, I'm not sure about that. Let's not get ahead of ourselves here. As I was telling Lia, we've only spent a little time together and it's far from anything serious. I really don't have time for much more than that right now anyways. Now, not to change the subject, but how about let's—" She laughed. "Lia, let's talk about your love life or lack thereof."

Now it was Lia's turn to choke on her wine. "*My* love life? Well, that's a very boring topic. Not even worth mentioning, in fact." She noticed Gigi and Douglas exchanging a look. "Now, what's that, you two? You really need to cool it on the secretive looks, which are really not quite so discreet." Lia laughed, hoping to lighten the mood, which suddenly seemed to be going in a more serious direction.

Douglas cleared his throat, as he often did when he was slightly uncomfortable about what he was about to say. Lia had come to know this about him.

"Well, we were wondering—about Ari's birth father."

Gigi said, "We know it's none of our business, but Ari did share with me a few things that you had told her about her father. It was lovely really. Please don't be angry."

"I'm not angry." Lia sighed. "It's just an absurd thing to think about, really. It was ages ago, and Antonio doesn't know anything about me." Lia looked down, trying to hide the tears that had suddenly sprung up. "He doesn't even know anything about Arianna." Lia couldn't hold back the sob that was caught in her throat. *What kind of person does that? He didn't deserve any of that.* "I should have told him, regardless of the circumstances." Lia's voice was very quiet. "Maybe things could have been different, if I'd told him all those years ago, but it's too late now."

"But what if it's not too late?" Gigi said quietly.

"Sometimes we're allowed second chances in life," Douglas said as he tenderly looked at Gigi beside him.

"You did have a second chance with Ari," Blu said. "Maybe Antonio still thinks about you. Young love can be quite powerful, and from what Ari told us, it seems that you two never really fell out of love when you left Italy."

Lia was taking it all in as she dried her tears on her napkin. "The thing is, I know he's moved on. When I was there before to visit my parents—before they passed away—I did ask about him. He had moved to Rome and he was engaged, so it's not as if I haven't thought about him. But yes, it's too late for us. And besides, what would I even say to him about Ari? The thought terrifies me, quite honestly. I doubt he could ever forgive me for that." Lia sighed, because she knew that it was something she'd never be able to make amends for. Another cross for her to bear and a reason for the guilt that always seemed to be there, haunting her, just under the surface of any happiness that touched her.

Gigi was nodding her head slowly. "I'm sorry that we've upset you, tonight of all nights. It's time to enjoy this dinner and our last evening together until Tuscany." Gigi raised her glass as she spoke. "Here's to Lia and her big adventure ahead."

The others raised their glasses and smiled as they toasted their friend.

CHAPTER 7

Lia woke up early the next morning and, as she pulled the heavy down comforter closer around her, had to think for a moment where she was. She had stayed in this room upstairs, just down the hall from Arianna's, many times.

She got up, crossed the room, and opened the curtains, taking in the first early morning signs of the day to come. She smiled as she saw the spectacular bridge in the distance through the misty morning haze that enveloped it.

Sitting in the comfortable chair by the window reminded her of the first night she'd spent here with Arianna. They'd sat together admiring the view as Arianna told her bits and pieces about her childhood here, how she'd come to really appreciate the home and life her parents had created for them. Even then, she knew they were growing closer, as Arianna was finally opening up to her about the things that had first seemed off limits, the things that would only serve as a reminder to Lia of what she'd lost when she signed away her rights all those years ago.

Lia got up and walked quietly down the hallway until she stood in front of Arianna's door. Her heart pounding, she slowly turned the knob, entered, and quietly shut the door behind her. She couldn't help the sharp intake of breath that followed as she took in the room, the place where she'd last seen her daughter alive.

She walked over to sit on the carefully made bed, the decorative pillows arranged just the way Ari anna had liked. She smoothed the bedspread and let herself lie back against the pillows in the hopes that she could smell her daughter's perfume, in the hopes that the memories that came flooding back would be happy ones and not of their last goodbye.

But it was hard to have good memories here, in this room, where Arianna had taken her last breath. All at once Lia felt a flutter of something deep inside. It was as if Arianna was reminding her of where the best memories were—and to follow them.

Lia smiled because she knew that her leaving was what her daughter would have wanted. She would refuse to be sad and would look forward to the memories of their time together in Italy.

Italy. She couldn't believe that she was finally making the trip today. It *had* been a long time coming, and her friends were right in their pushing of it, even though Lia still felt unsure about it all. But she was going. There was no backing out now.

She looked up suddenly, hearing a small tap at the door.

"Come in."

"Ah, I though it might be you I heard," Gigi said, entering the room. "Are you okay?"

Lia noticed the worried crease on her friend's forehead. "*Sì*, yes, I'm fine. Just getting a little lost in memories, you know?"

Gigi came over to sit on the bed next to Lia. "Yes, I do know. I've spent a bit of time in this room myself over the past year. It's still strange to me. Sometimes when I come up here, I *almost* forget as I wait to knock on the door. It's still hard to believe all of the loss this house has seen." Gigi's voice grew quieter. "Sometimes I'm not sure if it's right being here, if I'm being honest."

Lia looked at her friend and wondered about the things that maybe she hadn't been telling her. On the surface, it seemed that she was doing well, and Lia suspected that her love affair with Douglas had helped her a lot through her grieving process. But it would be hard to live here in this house with all of the memories. And even more so for Gigi, who hadn't lost just Arianna, but the entire family that she had looked after for so many years.

Lia reached out to take her friend's hand. "I'm sorry, Gigi. I've been so wrapped up in my own feelings that I'm afraid I've not been a good friend to you lately. Of course it must be hard for you here. I can't even begin to imagine."

Gigi was quiet, and Lia guessed that she was trying to be careful of the words she chose.

"It's not so much how hard it is. It is hard sometimes, but having Douglas here helps, and Ari had taken so much care in planning everything that I know there's no issue with the fact of the house being given to me."

Lia nodded in agreement.

"It's just that I don't know what the future is for Douglas and me here. It won't be long before he's thinking about retirement; and quite honestly, most days I don't quite know what to do with myself, putzing around this big house alone. I've actually been contemplating getting a job with another family, but Douglas doesn't like the idea."

"Do you think it's something that would make you feel good?" said Lia, knowing full well the odd feeling of suddenly not having to work; she had been struggling with this herself over the past year. Taking care of people was something Gigi and Lia had in common. They'd both worked at managing the households of other, wealthy people for years. It was what they knew. And abandoning it was a hard adjustment to wrap one's head around at times.

"I do in some regards, but I also understand what I think is turning into real frustration for Douglas. He's a proud man and he wants to take care of me. Well, he knows that Ari has left me in a good place financially; but more than that he just wants me to be the one taken care of for once, I think." Gigi laughed, and Lia got the sense that the shift in her expression was a bit forced.

"Oh, enough about all of this. Douglas and I will figure it all out. We've got plenty of time." Gigi grinned. "Now how about a fresh batch of scones and some nice Italian coffee? The one thing that I can confidently treat you to."

Lia smiled and got up off the bed. "Your scones are as delicious as anything I've had in Italy, and I thought you'd never ask. I'll come to the kitchen with you."

The two women made their way to the door, and there Lia turned for one last look around the room. She couldn't help but feel that she might not be seeing this room or this house again. It wouldn't be something she'd ever fault Gigi for, but she felt the need to emotionally prepare herself for the possibility. She took a deep breath, closed the door quietly and made her way downstairs to the kitchen.

Shortly after she was settled at the breakfast table with Gigi, Lia heard shouts coming from the guest room down the hall. "What's that all about?" she asked Gigi, who was shaking her head in what looked like disapproval.

"I'm telling you, I do love that child, but I have my fears that Blu has a problem on her hands if she doesn't do something soon. The last few times that I've seen her, I've noticed a change in her attitude; and if you ask me, she's too young to start going down that road. She used to be very respectful of her mother and suddenly she's lost a lot of that."

Lia nodded. "Blu touched on that with me the other night, but we didn't really get a chance to get into it. Do you suppose it's just all of the changes, what with the move to San Diego and everything? I would have thought that Jemma would adjust pretty well to living there, from what I've heard about how much she loved her times at the beach house."

"Oh, I don't know that the change in location is necessarily the issue, although I'm sure it could be part of it." Gigi looked thoughtful as she continued. "I suppose it probably has a lot to do with how hard Blu's been pushing to complete her clothing line. Jemma's probably not used to having to share so much of the time that the two of them used to spend alone together. Blu did work a lot when she lived here, but anytime she wasn't working, she was with her. I'm not sure that it's the same now. Or at least Jemma probably sees her around home and her studio a lot but the attention is more divided on Blu's part. Between you and me, I get the feeling that Blu is feeling pretty stressed and overwhelmed these days."

"It's the same thought I'd been having," Lia said, lowering her voice when she saw Blu walking in their direction from down the hall.

"Morning, sunshine," Lia said to Blu, who was looking more than a little frazzled as she reached for a coffee mug.

"The rebels are up. That's for sure." Blu laughed. "That child of mine."

"What's going on?" asked Gigi. "Anything I can help you with?"

"No, thanks. She'll be okay. She's just angry about having to head back home tonight. For some reason, she has it in her head that it's perfectly okay to miss the next week of school and that I should take off from work to play hooky with her while we are away." Blu laughed again, but Lia noticed that she did look more stressed out than usual.

"Well, put the hammer down," said Gigi. "As much as I'd love to have you both here for the week, the child needs to be in school."

Blu sighed. "To be honest, I've been thinking of pulling her out of school and hiring someone to come in to teach her. A private tutor of sorts, who can also travel with us."

Lia's eyes met Gigi's over her sip of coffee. "Hmm." It was out of her mouth before she could even realize it.

"What's hmm?" Blu said, and Lia thought she detected more than a bit of annoyance in her tone. "Do you think it's a horrible idea? Honestly, it's that or I'm going to have to hire a nanny, which I'm even more reluctant to do."

Lia knew how protective Blu had always been when it came to Jemma. Arianna had shared with her that it was one of those things that she just didn't push with her best friend, that in the years that Ari had known her, she could easily count on one hand the people that Blu had trusted to spend time caring for her daughter. And Lia had seen that as well during the time she knew them.

"Oh, I'm sorry. Don't mind me," Lia said quickly. "I'm obviously the last person to give advice about parenting." The remark seemed to sting everyone sitting at the table, and now Lia felt bad for taking the conversation in this direction. It wasn't how she wanted to leave them all this morning.

Blu was quick to give Lia a hug. "No, no worries at all. I'm sure that I need to think about it more. And I'm not giving up, in terms of figuring out this attitude of hers that seems to need a little adjustment these days. It's just that with my new clothing line coming out in a few months, I have a lot of shows lined up—that means either I'm taking Jemma with me or she's going to have to stay behind with someone, a thought which terrifies me, quite honestly."

Lia hugged her back. "I'm sure that you'll work it out, and you know that I—" She looked at Gigi, who was nodding in agreement. "—that we are here for you if you need to talk, vent, or bounce some ideas around. Well, I'll be a phone call away, I should say, but definitely available to you—to both of you." Lia was shocked at the tears that suddenly threatened. "Oh God. What am I doing, moving so far away from the only real friends I have?"

Gigi laughed and hugged her close. "Oh, don't be silly. We're going to be fine and so are you. *And* we can't wait to see you in Italy in just a few months. I'm already imagining the trip and all of the gorgeous food you're gonna feed me in that lovely little restaurant of yours."

Blu was nodding her head in emphatic agreement. "It's all that Jemma's been talking about. Actually, I need to remind her about the time off from school she'll be taking when we go. Maybe that will be reason enough for her to pipe down about school tomorrow. Thanks for the reminder. And, I totally agree with everything Gigi just said. We'll all be fine. Better than fine, really. Especially you, Lia. I already can't wait to talk to you about your new home."

It was Blu's turn to reach over to Lia for a big hug as the women finished their coffee. Lia got up to go find Jemma for a goodbye hug before she was due to leave. Douglas had popped his head in earlier to say that they'd be leaving for the airport in just a bit, so Lia knew that it was time to start saying her goodbyes.

PAULA KAY

CHAPTER 8

It seemed all too quickly that Douglas was putting Lia's luggage in his car; and Lia, walking arm-in-arm with Gigi, Jemma hovering at her leg, was ready to say her final goodbyes. There was no brushing the tears aside at this point, as they were now flowing freely. Even Jemma was sobbing into Lia's sweater as the adult pried the young girl's hands from around her waist to hoist her up to eye level.

"Don't you cry, sweetie. You're gonna come see me real soon, right?"

Jemma wiped at her face as she turned to glance at Blu, who was nodding her head and crying too. "Yes. We'll come see you real soon. We promise. Right, Mommy?" The child turned once again to get the assurance from Blu.

"That's right. We'll be seeing Lia again in no time at all. Now give her one last squeeze so that the rest of us can have a turn." Blu and Gigi laughed as they both reached to hug Lia at the same time.

Lia placed her arm around Blu's shoulder and

whispered in her ear, "Everything's gonna be just fine. Jemma will be fine." She kissed her cheek and then tried to make what she hoped was a stern expression. "And missy, you and I have lots yet to discuss. I feel like we didn't even make a dent in all of the questions I have for you—namely that I saw that write-up in the San Diego paper, and I'm dying to know how everything is going."

Blu grinned and gave Lia one final big hug. "Business is booming, as they say. I, on the other hand, feel like I could sleep for about a week straight."

"Well, you are welcome to come visit whenever you like." Lia turned to Gigi and Douglas; he had now come up to join the little party. "That goes for you two, as well. I know that you are planning to visit Gigi's family in the south when you come, but you're always welcome to some extra weeks in Tuscany. I'd love to have you there."

Douglas looked at his watch. "*That* is a wonderful offer, and one that we will certainly be considering, but now I'm afraid that we have to get on the road if you're going to make that flight."

He winked and kissed Gigi quickly. "Go on and get your last hug in, and I will call you later."

Gigi, wiping her eyes with the tissue she had balled up in her hand, reached over to give Lia one final big hug. "I'm going to miss you so much."

"I'm going to miss you too," Lia said, sniffling and struggling to hold back her own tears. "You've become such a dear friend to me. I want you to know that."

"I do know that. And the same is true for me. As much as I selfishly want to keep you here, I know it's time for you to go. We'll see you very soon." Gigi pointedly turned Lia's body round to face the door, giving her a little push. "Now go, before Douglas has to come back and pry you out of my arms."

Lia laughed, turned and blew one last kiss at the two women and Jemma.

"*Arrivederci!*"

Lia wiped the last of her tears as Douglas pulled away from the house. She saw him glance at her, and she thought she should try to pull herself together so that they could have at least a somewhat normal conversation.

"You'll be back, Lia. And we'll come to see you before you know it."

"I know. I'll be okay." Lia looked at Douglas and put her tissue away in her pocket. "It's just another change. I should be used to it by now."

"Oh, I don't know. Does one ever *really* get used to such big changes? You've been through a lot. Don't be so hard on yourself. If I could be so bold in saying it, if there's one thing I want for you, Lia, it's to stop knocking yourself around so much. I get the feeling that you do that a lot."

Lia couldn't help but smile despite the discomfort that she felt anytime someone tried to talk to her about such personal things. But Douglas was different than even Gigi or Blu. For some reason, ever since she'd first contacted him about Arianna all those months ago, she felt a real peace about trusting him. She always felt that he only wanted the best for Arianna and now, thankfully, she felt that he thought the same about her. She was lucky to have such good people in her life.

"I appreciate your concern," Lia responded after she had collected her thoughts. "And you're right. I am hard on myself and I suppose it's something that I should become more conscious of. Maybe I need to learn a thing or two about forgiveness. Of myself, I mean, and yada, yada, yada." She tried unsuccessfully to lighten the mood.

"Yep," said Douglas.

Lia imagined that he had a lot more to say on the matter, but was restraining his words at the moment.

"So, you have your ticket? Your passport?" said Douglas. "I suppose I should have asked you that before we pulled out of the driveway." He laughed.

"Yes, I do. And about that ticket."

Douglas glanced over at her, nodding his head. "Yes?"

"I switched the seat from first to economy class. So you'll have a refund to your card for the difference," Lia said quickly.

"And why did you do that?" Douglas said. "I really thought that you'd learned to enjoy the comforts of first class travel after your trip with Ari—after your last trip to Italy." He smiled as if to show Lia that he was teasing her.

"I did, and it was the first time that I'd ever *not* flown economy. And it was very special actually—with Ari. I don't know. It just seemed odd to me. A bit frivolous, I guess. Does that make sense?"

Douglas didn't answer right away, as he seemed to be choosing his words carefully. "It does. Yes. But you know that you can afford it now. We all can afford it. And I wasn't worried, buying you that ticket." He glanced over to her and smiled.

"Oh, I know. And I get what you are saying. I'll get there." She laughed and was pleased to hear Douglas laughing with her. "In time."

"I know you will, Lia. Just don't wait too long." He winked at her and they continued the rest of the drive in easy silence, Lia lost in her own thoughts and Douglas seeming to know that she needed the silence just then.

Douglas pulled up to departures, and Lia was pleased to see that she had plenty of time to get herself checked in.

"Are you sure that you don't want me to park and help you with your bags? I have plenty of time before my first client meeting this morning," said Douglas.

"Oh no, I'll be fine if we can just get my bags onto one of those carts." Lia gestured to the luggage carts a few feet away, and Douglas was immediately off to pull one up to the car. "Besides, I'm sure that you have plenty of other 'lawyerly' type things to attend to." Lia smiled.

"Oh, you mean like playing golf and attending

overpriced lunches?"

Douglas laughed, and it reminded Lia how much she always enjoyed his sense of humor. He was the first lawyer she had actually known so well, and she had been pleasantly surprised that he didn't live up to any of the stereotypes that she'd grown up believing.

"Yeah, something like that." Lia laughed too and reached up to give Douglas a big hug. "Thank you so much for the ride. And for everything, really." She took a deep breath. "I am not going to cry any more. Or at least not until I'm seated on the plane." They both laughed. "But I feel like I owe you a lot. You and Gigi. You've been such good friends to me." She looked Douglas in the eye as she spoke.

"You owe us nothing. The same should be said—and is said—about you, my dear. You are a good friend to us and we're lucky to have you in our lives. And that is not changing just because of a few miles." He winked. "Now scoot. Before you miss your flight."

They shared one final quick hug and then Lia was off to find her check-in desk. It was happening. And she was ready for it. At least she thought she was, even as she was fighting those last bits of doubt that she was slightly worried might never leave her. But she'd been fighting doubts all her life. It was something she was used to. It was only the niggling idea in the back of her mind that maybe, just maybe, it was time to be done with that. Sometimes she swore that what she thought was the strangest of ideas was actually Arianna's voice she was hearing. Even the thought of it now made her smile as she waited at the gate for her row to be called for boarding.

PAULA KAY

CHAPTER 9

Before long, Lia was making her way to the window seat that she'd carefully chosen a few days ago. She liked being able to rest her head near the window and look out at the world literally passing her by.

She got herself adjusted, and within a few moments the seat next to her was being occupied. There was a game she used to play every time she flew—trying to guess the story of the people sitting around her. It was always so interesting to think about the randomness of life, sitting in one place with all these different people who had only their departure city and destination in common.

Sometimes she would speak to the person sitting next to her, but often she liked to keep to herself when she flew. Truth be told, she hadn't flown that much really; and whenever she did, there was something major going on in her life, so she had lots to think about as the miles spread out beneath her. She looked around and couldn't help but wonder if anyone saw her on this plane and wondered about *her* life. Or what they'd think about her if they did know the details of her life.

Before Lia had much time to cry again or think about what was happening, the instructions had been given by the flight attendant and they were in the air. She laid her head back against the seat and closed her eyes. Maybe now she could really process what was happening in her life, with no distractions, ends to tie up, or people to see. She sighed. She *should* be more excited—elated, in fact. Who wouldn't be? She'd been given the chance of a lifetime to fulfill her dream. All she'd ever wanted, since she was a little girl cooking dinners with her grandmother in Tuscany, was to be a chef and ultimately to have her own restaurant. She smiled despite the inner scolding she was giving herself for being such a brat. She *was* excited about Thyme. She would make this work. It was what Arianna wanted for her.

"Are you staying in Florence?"

The pleasant voice of the woman sitting next to her interrupted Lia's thoughts.

"Oh, I'm sorry. I didn't realize that you were sleeping," she said when Lia's eyes popped open and she turned slightly in her chair, even though the thought had crossed her mind that she should pretend to be asleep. She wasn't sure yet if she was up for conversation so soon after take-off. It was going to be a long flight, and there were plenty of things that she wanted to sort through in her mind.

Lia smiled at the woman sitting next to her, despite

her initial resistance. She had a great smile and the most gorgeous curly red hair. "Not to worry. I wasn't asleep. I'm going on from Florence to a town in Chianti."

"I'm actually going to Chianti as well. I live there—in Greve. Are you visiting Tuscany?"

"I'll be in Castellina in Chianti—I'm moving there," Lia said, recognizing that she wasn't being overly friendly or inviting conversation, but unable to stop herself. She wasn't sure yet of her mood.

"Oh, you are only about a thirty-minute drive from me." The woman reached out her hand to Lia. "I'm Rebecca, by the way."

"Good to meet you. I'm Lia." She shook Rebecca's hand and felt her resistance disappearing. Perhaps they were destined to be friends; God knew that Lia could use a friend in the near future. She wasn't sure if she would feel lonely in Italy, but she'd grown used to her easy friendship with Gigi and she imagined that she'd be missing that a lot.

"I'm sorry, Rebecca. I don't mean to be so short with you. I've just had a lot on my mind—and—well, I'm not really sure how I'm feeling right now about this trip, to be honest."

"Oh, you'll love Tuscany. I can promise you that," Rebecca said with such exuberance in her voice that it was hard to doubt her. "I've lived there for six months now—with my husband." She grinned as only a newlywed could.

"I grew up there, actually," said Lia, making the mental decision to engage a bit with this friendly woman sitting next to her. "So, I guess it's sort of a homecoming for me. Is your husband Italian, then?"

"Yes, my husband—Marco—is from the region as well. I met him when I first came to Italy about a year ago." A funny expression crossed Rebecca's face as she continued. "God, I can't believe that it's only been a year. Funny how much things can change in a year." She laughed, and Lia was intrigued enough to want to hear more of the woman's story.

"Were you there on vacation then? When you met your husband?"

"Well, it sounds silly to say but I was having a bit of a crisis, in fact. I call it my 'Eat, Pray, Love' period."

Lia nodded her head to show her understanding of the book reference. "Well, it certainly sounds as though it was a good move on your part." She smiled at Rebecca, noticing how genuinely happy the woman seemed.

"Oh, yes. I wouldn't change a thing. At the time, I was feeling so stuck. I'd been divorced for about a year and was really having a hard time getting past it. Finally, I just decided to sell my house, pack up my bags, and go to Italy to take a cooking class. Best decision I've ever made." Rebecca laughed.

"You like to cook, then?" Lia asked, thinking it pretty great that they already had this one thing in common.

"Oh well, yes. I do *like* to cook. Now, am I good at it?

That's another story entirely." Rebecca laughed. "Marco teases that his mother will give me cooking lessons because she is so worried about him not getting enough to eat."

Lia laughed at the comment, because she was well aware of the doting antics of an Italian mother when it came to her sons.

"I do love Italian food, though. And unfortunately I am paying for that." Rebecca pointed to her stomach comically. "I've put on twenty pounds since I arrived, and I really do need to get that under control. My husband says that he likes a little extra padding, but good grief— Italian women are so thin and gorgeous. I'm not sure that I completely buy it, so I'm going to be working on getting this weight off right away."

Lia thought Rebecca looked fine, but she couldn't really relate to the idea of wanting to look good for a man. It had been so long since she'd even thought about dating—since she had even felt a man was the least bit interested in her. But then again, she'd not been putting any vibes out about being available either. She sighed. She really didn't see that changing in the near future. She was more interested in the restaurant than anything, really.

Lia suddenly remembered the woman sitting next to her and silently reprimanded herself for being rude. "I'm sure that your husband does appreciate you just the way you are." She smiled at Rebecca. "And speaking of Italian food, I actually am going to Castellina because I own a restaurant there." She smiled, hearing herself say this for the first time out loud.

The look that crossed Rebecca's face was priceless. "You do? Which restaurant? My husband and I go there quite often, actually."

"It's a small place, near the town center. It's called Thyme."

"Are you kidding? We love that place. I can't wait to tell my husband."

Lia smiled at her reaction. "How funny. I can't believe that you've eaten there. Yes, I'm a chef myself and this is kind of a new thing for me. No, actually it's a *completely* new thing for me." Lia laughed, but inside she was thinking about the complexity of explaining the whole situation to a complete stranger, and she didn't know if she was up for that.

"Wow. I can't believe this either. How did you come to own that restaurant and how long have you had it? I really thought that the cook we met—Carlo, I think his name was—*was* the owner."

"He was—he has been." Lia sighed and just decided to be honest. "It's kind of a long story."

"It's okay. I understand long stories. Believe me." Rebecca laughed. "We can save it for another day—if you think that'd be alright? I'd love to come in some time to eat and to have a good chat once you're settled."

"I'd really love that," said Lia, thinking that she actually would look forward to seeing Rebecca again. She had a strong feeling that she was someone that Lia could be friends with and even though she didn't feel like talking much now, she knew there might come a time in the near future when she could use the listening ear of a good girlfriend.

"I think I should maybe have a nap now. I'm just realizing how emotionally drained I'm feeling after all of my goodbyes this morning. Suddenly, I'm exhausted."

"You sleep then. I won't bother you." Rebecca smiled. "I have the feeling that there will be plenty of time later for conversation."

Lia adjusted her pillow, leaned her seat back, and fell asleep for the better part of the remaining flight.

PAULA KAY

CHAPTER 10

Before she knew it, Lia was awoken from her fitful sleep by the flight attendant asking her to put her seat up in preparation for landing. She collected her belongings and said goodbye to Rebecca with the promise of seeing her very soon in the restaurant.

Lia was a little bit annoyed at herself for sleeping the whole trip, as she would now probably have to deal with a serious case of jet lag as she worked to adjust to the new time zone. She did have sleeping pills that her doctor had prescribed much earlier in the year, so she'd use them if she had any problems after the first couple of days or so.

She made her way through immigration and customs, and then collected her bags, all with no problems. She'd booked a driver to take her from the airport to Castellina; she saw him holding up the sign with her name on it right outside of the luggage collection. So far, so good, she thought. And she really hadn't had much time to think about things since shortly after boarding the plane. The sleep may have actually been the best thing for her.

Once she was settled in the car, she sat back to take in

the beautiful countryside for the nearly one-hour drive to the guest house where she'd be staying. When they were arranging her trip, Douglas had wanted to book her a nice villa just outside of town. But she'd thought it best to stay at one of the local inns near the restaurant to make it easy upon her arrival. She promised him that she'd start looking at places to eventually buy shortly after, and he'd volunteered to help her when it came to the paperwork and the many financial pieces that needed to be put in order. He and Gigi were constantly reminding her that there was more than enough money there for her to buy a nice home that she'd be comfortable in. To Lia, it seemed a huge step, never having owned her own home before. So she'd convinced him to book her in the inn, promising to settle in quickly thereafter.

As she watched the beautiful Tuscan countryside out her window, she couldn't stop the memories from washing over her. The last time she was here and had taken the exact same ride from Florence to her new home, Arianna had filled the car with laughter and her wide smile, so happy and carefree to finally be in Italy. Lia had loved sharing those moments with her daughter. She could hardly believe that she was back here now alone. She sighed and tried very hard to hold back the tears. *How long was she going to cry? To grieve?* Was moving to Italy going to help her or make the pain of losing Arianna worse? She didn't know how it could possibly get any worse than what she'd felt over the course of the last year; but being here now, with the memories rushing back, she wondered if she'd made a big mistake in coming.

Before she knew it they were driving through Castellina, and everything was as she remembered it. The quaint village where she had grown up hardly seemed to have changed to her, or maybe she just wasn't sure if she wanted to see the changes. It was just getting to be dusk, and the colors of the evening sky against the old architecture were beautiful. For a moment, she started to feel some of the old excitement deep down inside, teasing her that maybe she was just starting her journey back. She could almost hear Arianna's voice in her ear. *Isn't it beautiful? Look at that Italian sky. I've waited my entire life to see a sky like this.* And Lia thought that maybe she should remember and listen to her daughter. Maybe, just maybe, her entire life had been leading her to this place and moment in time.

She stepped out of the car after the driver pulled up beside the lovely old inn that Lia had chosen. She'd made the selection based on its proximity to the restaurant, thinking that she'd want to jump right in, her first week there, and it'd be best if she could walk to and from the inn until she found herself a house and got proper transportation. She didn't know yet if she wanted to buy a place in town or venture out into the countryside a bit. There would be time for that later. She was not making any major decisions just yet.

Before she had a chance to knock on the front door,

an older Italian woman appeared, to give her a kiss on each cheek and greet her as only the Italian women can do.

"*Buonasera*, you are Lia, *si?*"

"*Si.*" Lia smiled and took the woman's hand, telling her in Italian that it was wonderful to be there.

"I am Elena. We're pleased to have you. Come follow me. I will show you to your room." A man had appeared to collect her bags from the driver of Lia's car, and Elena gestured towards him. "This is my husband, Franco."

Lia instantly felt at home. She followed the woman to her room, which she soon discovered was quite lovely. It was a good size, with a separate sitting room and full bathroom attached. Elena disappeared and was back a few minutes later with a tray of cheeses, meats, and bottled water. "Would you like some wine?" Elena asked.

"No, *grazie*. This will be fine," said Lia, thinking that she was suddenly starving and that the tray of food looked delicious.

Elena turned to her before leaving. "You need anything, come let us know. There is a bell in the front hallway. Whenever you wake, come down to the dining room in the morning for coffee and breakfast."

"*Grazie*, Elena. Everything looks wonderful," Lia said, holding back a yawn and wondering how she could be so tired after sleeping so much on the plane. She hadn't slept for several nights that past week, so she suspected it was all catching up to her now. She would have a bit of food and then crawl into bed, ready to face the day ahead tomorrow. She was relieved to find that she was feeling quite positive, and even excited about exploring a bit in the morning. She *had* dreamed of living back in Italy her whole adult life after all. Maybe she needed to pinch herself and realize how lucky she was.

PAULA KAY

CHAPTER 11

Lia slept soundly in her new bed, awaking to the delicious smell of strong Italian coffee. She made her way downstairs, where she found Elena organizing a tray of beautiful croissants and other delicious-looking baked goods. She looked up as Lia entered the room.

"*Buongiorno*, Lia. How did you sleep?" Elena asked.

"*Buongiorno*. Very well, *grazie*. The bed is very comfortable."

"Let me make you a coffee, and help yourself to a croissant."

"*Sì*, they look and smell delicious," said Lia, placing one on her plate.

"We are lucky." Elena smiled. "One of the town's best bakeries is just down the road."

"Ooh, good to know," said Lia, accepting the mug of coffee from Elena.

"So, what will you do today? Do you need some tips on things to see?"

"I've moved here, actually. It's not really a vacation."

"Really? How wonderful. You'll have to let Franco

and me know what we can do to help you get settled. We have you booked for the week. Is that right?"

"*Si*, I need to get organized with Thyme—the restaurant nearby—and then I will begin looking for a place to live." She noticed the confused look on Elena's face.

"The restaurant? *Si*, it is one of our favorites here in town," said Elena.

"I am the new owner—well, I have been for awhile, but Carlo has been running it for me until now. I will go over to see him there this morning, in fact."

"That's wonderful. I'm sure you'll find the town very welcoming," said Elena with a big smile.

"I'm sure I will." Lia thought that she'd tell Elena another time that she grew up here. She didn't think that she had the time this morning for a big conversation, and she wanted to get herself together to go see Carlo. He was expecting her arrival; they'd been communicating via phone calls ever since Douglas had organized the final paperwork and finances for the sale. Carlo had seemed relieved, and Lia couldn't help but wonder if Arianna's desire to gift it to her didn't in part have to do with helping out Carlo. The two had spoken several times during their visit to Tuscany, and Arianna was well aware of Carlo's financial situation with the restaurant. Things hadn't been easy for him once his wife had gotten sick, so the sale seemed to come at just the perfect time, he had told Lia later. Of course he was devastated to learn of

Arianna's passing.

Lia thanked Elena for her breakfast when she was finished, and headed upstairs to get ready to go out. She planned to have a little walk around the neighborhood before meeting Carlo at the restaurant around ten o'clock.

It was hard not to smile as she walked out the door minutes later, feeling the cool morning air touch her face. She was reminded of everything she loved in this little slice of heaven she would now get to call home. Maybe this move was exactly what she needed to get out of the funk she'd been in. God knew she needed something. It was hard to imagine that she could keep on living in the state she'd been in. Not that she'd contemplated ending her life or anything. That was something she would never do. She'd been through hardships enough to know that it would pass and that time would heal—although she, more than anyone, knew that healing didn't necessarily mean forgetting or even letting go. That was the part that she struggled with the most. But for the moment she was feeling positive, and anxious to see the restaurant again.

She took her time walking to the restaurant, wandering down the little lanes and into the squares that she remembered from her youth. It felt strange to be here now—by herself like this. It was as if any moment she was going to hear her father shouting at her from down the road to come in for dinner. She smiled, remembering those times. It was funny how being back in a place could transport one instantly to a different time period, one where life was happy and carefree, she thought.

She arrived at Thyme and smiled when she saw Sofia outside placing fresh flowers on the tables. The young girl looked up and then rushed over to greet her, kissing her on both cheeks.

"*Buongiorno*, Lia. We've been waiting for you," Sofia said with a huge grin on her face. "My uncle is inside. Come on, come in."

"It's so good to see you, Sofia." Lia had grown quite fond of the girl during her time in Tuscany a year ago. When the sale had been finalized, she was very pleased to know that Carlo and Sofia would both be interested in staying on to help her with the restaurant. She knew that she would need them, and seeing Sofia's cheerful disposition now was a good confirmation of that decision. She'd be very pleased, really, if she could eventually come and go as she liked at the restaurant, leaving Carlo in charge. They'd work out the details; she suspected that there would be some changes she'd like to make, which hopefully wouldn't be too hard for Carlo to handle.

She entered the restaurant, and even though she'd been inside several times before, the simple beauty of the place took her breath away. She nearly had to stop Sofia so that she could sit down for a minute and take it all in. The sudden recognition that she *owned* the place hit her again from nowhere, and she didn't quite know how to handle the mix of emotions. *Was this really happening?* She said a silent "thank you" in her head to Arianna as she crossed the room to greet Carlo, who was coming out of the kitchen, wiping his hands on the apron he wore.

His grin was wide as he greeted her with a kiss on each cheek. "*Buongiorno*, bella. Finally. You have arrive to Thyme." He laughed easily, and Lia was reminded of how much she had liked the gentle giant of a man. His love for food was apparent, and it carried into his careful attention to the customers who entered the restaurant every day.

"*Buongiorno*, Carlo. It's so wonderful to see you. And to be here. Finally." Lia smiled. "The place looks wonderful and it smells even better." She winked. "I can't wait to eat some of your pasta."

"*Si*, it is your pasta now," said Carlo. "And now, I can congratulate you in person. Of course, I never wanted to sell the restaurant, but Arianna made me an offer I couldn't refuse; and knowing it was you who would have it made everything better."

Lia hugged him and believed his words, even though she knew it couldn't have been easy for him to sell. "Well, I'm so pleased that you agreed to stay on here to help me. I couldn't do it without you—without both of you." She nodded towards Sofia, who smiled in response. "It's been a rough year, and as much as I don't like to admit it, I think I really need this change."

"*Si*, I'm so sorry about Arianna," said Carlo, his expression reflecting the pain he felt as he expressed his condolences to Lia. "We were all very shocked, you know. She seemed so healthy when she was here. I never would have guessed——" He stopped, noticing Lia's pained expression, and pulled her to him for a big hug. "It's going to be okay, bella. And we will help you with whatever you need."

Lia hugged him back, feeling so thankful that there were people here who seemed to care about her too. She made a mental note to really try to make this transition with the restaurant smooth for everyone, especially Carlo. She wanted to respect the way that he had been running things all these years and not try to make too many changes all at once. He was a dear man, and more than anything, she'd hoped that they would remain good friends for years to come.

"*Grazie*, Carlo. Your words mean a lot to me. And I'm so thankful that you agreed to stay on and help me with the restaurant. I really think we're going to make a good team." She smiled; Carlo was already walking towards the kitchen, gesturing for Lia to follow him.

Carlo handed her an apron. 'So, shall we get started making the pasta?"

Lia laughed, instantly feeling at home in the kitchen. "*Si*, let's do it."

Lia and Carlo worked side-by-side in the kitchen, and before she knew it an hour had passed and suddenly the orders were coming in for lunch. She was happy to see the place was busy, and made a mental note that she probably needed to hire a few more people, both for the front of the restaurant and the kitchen. They got through the lunch service, and Lia took the time to go out and greet some of the customers, as Sofia introduced her to many of their regulars. Although she did enjoy the little bits of conversation, it was the kitchen that Lia most enjoyed, and before long she was back in there asking Carlo where she could help. He seemed to be doing a great job handling things with his one sous-chef. They were a well-oiled team, from what Lia could tell.

They finished up the work together and then took three heaping plates out to a table near the front of the restaurant.

"Sofia, put the closed sign up so we can eat some lunch," Carlo called out to his niece, and once she did, the three sat down together to dine on the delicious meal.

"Ooh, this is very good, Carlo. I can't believe that I am going to be able to eat this every day." Lia laughed and patted her stomach. "I'm going to have to get a good exercise routine going right away, I'm afraid."

They all laughed and had some easy conversation with one another, Lia in her broken Italian—which did seem to be coming back quite fast, as she'd hoped—and Carlo and Sofia trying their best to sprinkle the English words that they knew into the conversation. When they were finished with lunch, Lia got up to clear the table, with Sofia quickly taking the dishes out of her hands.

"I can do it, Lia. You sit. I'm sure you two have things to talk about," said Sofia, making her way to the kitchen with the dishes.

"*Grazie*, Sofia."

Lia turned to Carlo. "I'm thinking that I will plan to come in every day this week, either for the lunch or dinner service—I'm sure I may have a bit of jet lag, so a full day might be a bit much to start with." Lia tried unsuccessfully to stifle a big yawn, and Carlo laughed.

"*Si*, it is fine, Lia. Whatever you like. Sofia and I will be here and the restaurant will carry on as usual. We have plenty of time to discuss plans and you can come in whenever it is good for you. Of course, I welcome your help in the kitchen anytime." Carlo smiled. "I enjoy cooking with you."

"Me too," said Lia, getting up to leave. "And thank you again for everything, Carlo. It really means a lot to me."

"*Si*, you're very welcome. I'm glad you're here now." Carlo got up also, giving Lia a quick hug. "You go home and have a nice rest. Come in later for dinner if you like. We shouldn't be too busy this evening. Or I will see you tomorrow."

Lia left the restaurant feeling tired, but good. She was suddenly very sleepy and decided to head straight back to the inn, rather than go for another little walk like she'd planned. There'd be time for that later. Right now her cozy bed was calling her.

Lia woke up from her afternoon nap expecting to feel refreshed as she opened her eyes; she made her way over to the window to draw the curtains back. The view outside was pretty spectacular. The inn had a small garden with a fountain and benches, where Lia noticed one of the couples she'd seen earlier at the inn. Beyond the grounds, she could see one of the bigger courtyards near the town center. It looked inviting enough and she thought about heading out for a walk, but the knot in her stomach took her by surprise.

She'd been feeling so good and positive ever since her arrival, and now all of a sudden she was feeling that same sense of dread—the overwhelming sadness that she'd felt every day, or so it seemed, for the past year or so. It was as if she'd just woken up in her apartment back in San Francisco, wondering what the heck to do with her life now that Arianna was gone. She sighed. She really needed to shake herself out of this depression. She was here to change her life, to make a fresh start with it all. Instead of going for her walk, she drew the curtains closed, crawled back under her covers, and cried herself to sleep again.

PAULA KAY

CHAPTER 12

The week passed slowly for Lia. She would get up to have some breakfast downstairs and eventually make her way to the restaurant before lunch; not because she felt like it at all, but because she felt that she owed it to Carlo to show up.

By the third day that she'd been working in the kitchen, Carlo found her with tears streaming down her face at one point. He pulled her aside, placed his hands on her shoulders, and looked straight into her eyes.

"Bella, I don't know you very well, but I know that you are not happy here."

Lia broke into sobs, and he hugged her to his chest.

"Lia, you're going to have to let go of it. All of it. Before, when you were here, you were so happy cooking with me in the kitchen. Your laughter as you cooked was a delight to me. Now I see only sadness in your eyes and you seem to be getting more sad every day."

Lia nodded her head against his chest. She knew that Carlos was right. The days had gotten progressively harder, and she barely knew what she was doing here anymore. She had to figure out if this was even the best thing for her at all. But she had no real alternative. She could go back to San Francisco, but in a lot of ways that felt like running away. How would things be any different there?

"I think you should go home. For the rest of the day, maybe the next few days, with no work, just taking care of yourself. Go out and enjoy the countryside. I think it would do you some good." Carlo looked at her again and smiled to show that he wasn't being stern but just concerned about her.

"You're right, Carlo. I'm sorry that I've been such a drag around here. I really do need to get it together."

"No need to be sorry. I'm only worried about you. We'll be fine here, and I will love to see you again in a few days. Go. Get some rest and refresh yourself."

Lia smiled at his words. She was lucky to have him here, looking out for her. She hugged both Carlo and Sofia before leaving with the promise of returning within a few days.

Lia took the long way back to the inn, wandering around some of the small streets and peeking in shop windows. She had to sort herself out. She'd go home for a nap and then maybe help Elena in the kitchen with the evening meal. It seemed like forever since she'd really enjoyed herself while cooking. She'd been cooking at Thyme, of course, but it was more that she was just going through the motions, not really getting lost in the food as she normally would. She couldn't help but laugh lightly. God, she was really in an awful state to not be enjoying her cooking. Arianna would not have understood that. The thought came and went, almost without her realizing it. She'd figure it out. She just needed a little more time. *And possibly a little more forgiveness.*

There it was. The thought that haunted her. She didn't need a therapist to tell her that she was wrestling with a huge amount of guilt. Guilt that she probably really needed to figure out how to let go of. She sighed. Why did everything feel so difficult?

She entered the inn and made her way up to the bed that had become a comfort to her lately. She crawled under the covers telling herself that she would sort it all out in her head soon—after a long nap.

Lia awoke a few hours later feeling groggy and disoriented. Suddenly famished, she made her way downstairs to see if she could help Elena out in the kitchen. Entering the room, she grabbed an apron that was hanging near the door, not waiting for an invitation to pitch in.

"Lia, I was just thinking maybe I'd come upstairs to check on you. You've been sleeping a lot, *sì*? Are you feeling okay?" said Elena.

Lia smiled at the older woman, thinking to herself how lucky she was having such concerned people in her life.

"*Si*, I'm okay. Just so very tired these days." She tried to smile, because the last thing she wanted at the moment was to share her depression with someone. "I'd love to help with dinner, if you don't mind?" She was already making her way to the cutting board to start on the salad that looked to be underway.

"*Si*, of course. But you can also just sit and talk with me if you like. I don't want you to feel like you have to work while you are here. We are supposed to be taking care of you, my dear." Elena laughed, and Lia noticed that being in the kitchen with Elena made her miss Gigi back home.

"No, it is good for me, really." She smiled broadly to reinforce her position. "I love to cook." *Well, normally I love cooking*, she thought.

The two women worked side-by-side, each lost in her own thoughts. Lia sipped the wine that Elena had poured for her, and she realized that she was almost feeling a sense of normality and happiness.

"Elena, I'd love to cook the dinner tomorrow night, if you don't mind? I can go shopping in the morning, and if it's okay I'll prepare my favorite pasta dish. It's been ages since I've made it and suddenly I have a real craving."

'*Si*, that would be lovely." Elena looked at her with an odd expression. "If you're sure. And of course I will help you. We can do it together."

"That would be great, *grazie*."

"No, it's I that should be thanking you. We've never

really had a guest pitch in to help with the meals." Elena laughed as Franco breezed through the kitchen to pour himself a glass of wine, stopping to taste the sauce his wife was preparing and giving her a quick pat on the behind.

"The only thing better than my lovely wife in the kitchen is two lovely women in the kitchen." Franco laughed and scooted out of the room before Elena could snap him with the towel she was holding.

"Men," Elena said, laughing. "Forgive me for prying, but is there someone special in your life?"

Lia's heart quickened briefly as she tried to think of how much to divulge. "No, I've been single for a long time. It's hard to imagine not being single, and at my age—well, let's just say that there aren't a lot of suitors lined up at my door." She laughed, hoping that Elena would drop the subject.

"Well, bella. You must get out more, no? You are not going to meet them stuck in your room all day." She glanced at Lia, who was trying not to look cross. "Ah, I'm sorry. It's none of my business, as you say. Please forgive me. It's just that you are so beautiful. Any man should be so lucky to escort you to dinner."

Lia smiled and gave Elena a quick hug. "It's okay. And please don't take my silence for anger. It's just been a hard year and, really, dating has been the last thing on my mind, I guess. But when I'm ready—maybe I will let you know, and you and Franco will have lots of amazing handsome Italian men to set me up with." Lia laughed and hoped that she had closed the subject.

Seemingly satisfied with Lia's response, Elena brought out the serving dishes, heaping the plates high with thinly sliced beef and thick home-made pasta. She filled another bowl with the sweet-smelling sauce that had been simmering on the stove and took the fresh bread out of the oven. Lia grabbed the salad and the two of them went out to the dining room, ready to call the few guests that were there to the table for dinner.

Lia loved the Italian way of life, especially when it came to food and eating. There was always more than enough food prepared, so that no matter who might stop by or what random stranger might get an invitation to dine, there was always plenty of food. And wine, she thought as Elena poured her a second glass.

The small group of them sat down to a dinner that ran well into the evening. Before she knew it, Lia was enjoying the conversation and feeling almost normal again. Perhaps Carlo had been right after all and she just needed a few "normal" days at home, sleeping, cooking, and getting at least a bit of exercise each day. It was funny that she thought of the inn as her home. She'd have to remember to have a conversation with Elena later about staying for at least another week, as she wasn't nearly ready to make decisions about a house just yet. She guessed it would be fine, as they didn't seem to be too busy at the moment; she felt that they would welcome her stay there for as long as she liked. She smiled again at her luck in choosing the inn as a place to stay.

The next day, Lia got up early, finally making the time for the morning walk that she'd been promising herself. When she returned home, she and Elena took the car to the big market for some food shopping for Lia's dinner that night. Lia loved the market and all of the fresh Italian ingredients that she preferred to use in her cooking. She was having so much fun that she forgot herself for the moment, something that hadn't happened a lot to her lately.

She really enjoyed Elena's company and hoped that the two women would continue to be friends after she moved out of the inn. Thinking about it now, though, caused her a slight feeling of anxiety. She brushed it aside. There'd be time for thinking about a place to live later. For now, she was content to stay at the inn among her new friends.

As promised, Elena was by her side in the kitchen all afternoon, as Lia prepared the evening meal. She was making tagliatelle bolognese, her favorite dish, and the two women were sipping a glass of Chianti. Lia smiled and then realized that the quick flash of memory that she had of her daughter brought her joy and not sadness for once.

She caught Elena staring at her out of the corner of her eye. "Bella, you look so happy. Here, in the kitchen. It is the place where you belong."

Lia laughed. "I am happy, Elena. *Grazie.*" She gave the woman a quick hug.

"I love having you here. I really do. But I can't help but think that maybe it's time for you to be back at the restaurant?" Elena said, and Lia thought she detected carefulness in her friend's voice. "You're such a good cook. I feel that we are keeping you from the world here at the inn." The two women laughed at her comment.

"Well, I don't know about the world, Elena." Lia smiled. "But perhaps you are right about Thyme. I should go back tomorrow. I'm ready, and it's not right that Carlo is there without me."

Lia felt that she had crossed a hurdle that night, sitting in the dining room enjoying the meal that she and Elena had prepared. She definitely felt ready to get back to work. At least she thought that she could now be at the restaurant without bursting into tears every ten minutes. Poor Carlo. She shook her head at what she must have been putting him through those last days she was there. He probably didn't know what to think, and she wouldn't blame him for being concerned about the restaurant and wondering if Lia was going to be able to keep the place. But she knew that it was what she wanted. Yes, she still did feel sad but she had to keep moving forward, and going in to the restaurant was the first step in making that happen. Lia went to bed that night with a new determination and a plan for the next day.

CHAPTER 13

When Lia walked into the restaurant the next morning, Sofia greeted her warmly with a hug, and a kiss on each cheek. "Lia, it's so good to see you. How are you doing?"

"And you, lovely girl." Lia smiled warmly at the beautiful waitress, who was always so pleasant to be around. "I'm well, *grazie*. How are you doing?"

"I'm doing very good too." Sofia said in the broken English that Lia found delightful. "It has been very busy."

"Well, I'm here to help today—and from now on." Lia smiled. "Is your uncle in the kitchen?"

"*Si*, he is starting on the pasta for the lunch crowd."

Lia made her way into the kitchen, grabbing an apron and making Carlo jump as she called out a big hello to him.

He laughed. "You startled me, but I am so happy to see you." He kissed her on the cheek and then stepped back for a moment. "You look happy and rested, *sì*?"

Lia smiled at his scrutiny, remembering the patience

he'd had to show during her first few days in the restaurant. She was determined not to put the poor man through her emotional distress again today.

"*Si*, I am, Carlo. You were right about my needing a few days off, and I think it was good for me. Very sorry to put you through my meltdown earlier in the week."

Carlo looked at her with a confused expression on his face. "Meltdown? I don't understand this word."

Lia laughed. "Meltdown. Crying, sobbing, losing my mind."

He nodded in understanding. "Ah, not to worry. I am happy that you are feeling better—and now we can get on with some cooking, *si*?"

"*Si*, I'm very happy to start in on the lunch service with you now," Lia said as she rolled up her sleeves and got to work with the dough that was lying on the table. "It is good to be here."

The two worked side-by-side, making the fresh pasta and working on the different sauces that Carlo had cooking on the stove. Lia thought that it did feel great to be back in the kitchen. She must always remember to turn to cooking when she wasn't quite feeling herself. How was it that she had even forgotten that?

Towards the end of lunch service, when it had slowed down quite a bit, Sofia entered the kitchen to let Lia know that there was someone there to see her.

"Is it Elena, from the inn?" Lia asked, sure that it must be her.

"No, not Elena. An American woman I think. With pretty red hair. And a very handsome Italian with her." Sofia laughed.

Lia walked to the sink to wash her hands, thinking that it would be good to see Rebecca again. She was ready for a little company, and she was happy that Rebecca had made the trip to come see her. She had quite enjoyed their brief conversation on the plane, and thought she might look forward to getting to know the woman who had also chosen to make Tuscany her home.

Lia walked up behind Rebecca as she said a cheerful hello. Rebecca turned to give her a big hug, and the man beside her turned towards Lia as well.

"Lia, it's so good to see you." Rebecca smiled brightly. "This is my husband, Marco. Marco, this is Lia."

Lia and Marco reached for one another's hands, a sudden look of recognition passing between them. Lia felt sick and willed herself to speak normally.

"Lia, is it really you?" Marco asked, his eyes wide; Rebecca looked puzzled beside him.

"Marco, wow." Lia tried to find her voice. "It's been so long."

"Wait a minute. You two know each other? How?" Rebecca chimed in, looking completely shocked herself.

Marco turned towards his wife. "You know my cousin Antonio?"

Rebecca nodded.

"Lia and Antonio went together when we were

young."

Rebecca nodded her head. "Oh wow. That's a crazy coincidence. Funny that we didn't put that together on the plane."

Lia found her voice. "I know you said your husband's name was Marco, but it just never really occurred to me. Have a seat, please." Lia gestured towards the table, feeling like she needed to have a seat. And possibly a stiff drink.

"How is it that you are here, Lia? I mean, Rebecca told me that you are running Thyme now?" Marco said.

"Oh, that's a long story. Maybe for another time," Lia added. "But yes, I am here to run the restaurant," she said carefully.

"And Antonio? Have you spoken to him?"

"No, no, Marco. Not for many years." Lia could hear her voice growing quieter. "Actually not since I left for America when we were young."

She hardly knew what to say and was trying to act normal. "When I came back one time—it was when my father was ill. I'd heard that he was getting married, so I never tried to contact him. How is he doing?" she asked, just because it seemed the polite thing to say.

"No, he never got married." Marco said.

Lia's heart caught in her throat, not knowing if the news she was hearing was good or bad.

"He's been living in Rome for years, but—actually he's moving back here," Marco said suddenly, reaching for his phone. "I will give you his number. You should phone him. He'd be so surprised to hear from you." Marco grinned widely.

"No, no. Please don't tell him I'm here, Marco." The words sounded slightly panicked, even to Lia's ear, but she couldn't stop them. She noticed the perplexed look on Rebecca's face. "It's just that—well, I have so much to take care of right now. I'm not quite ready to speak to him," she tried to explain, knowing that the words sounded silly.

"But Lia. He would love to see you. I know he would. We speak quite often, and he's wondered about you over the years."

Marco seemed so sure of his words, which made Lia panic even more. God, she wasn't ready to see Antonio at all. She didn't know if she ever would be, but now that she knew his circumstances, she felt the dread of the inevitable. There would come a day where she'd have to tell him about her past. About Arianna. The thought filled her with terror and she felt physically sick to her stomach. She turned to Rebecca, hoping that she could convey the importance of what she was saying by the look on her face.

"Please promise me that you won't tell him—not yet. I will speak to him soon. I will," she said to Marco, but it was Rebecca who reached out to her.

"Don't worry, Lia. We won't mention anything." She turned pointedly to Marco. "And we'll keep our nose out of your business as well. Right, honey?"

Marco nodded and kissed Rebecca lightly on the lips. "If you say so, but every day I grow more confused by you—you women."

Lia and Rebecca laughed, and Lia was thankful for the change of tone in the conversation.

"Now, have you two eaten? What can I get for you?" Lia asked, wanting to return to the kitchen to collect her thoughts.

"We've ordered from the waitress already. Our favorite pasta dish," Rebecca said.

Lia got up from the table. "I'll just go check on that for you." She motioned for Sofia. "Sofia will bring you some bread and get your drinks."

Lia rushed off to the kitchen, thankful for the distraction. She took a few deep breaths, trying to collect her thoughts and emotions, as she felt that she was about to pass out from the shock of the news that she'd heard.

She always knew in the back of her mind that one day she might run into Antonio again. Even though she knew his parents had also passed away a few years ago, he came from a big family, and it wasn't reasonable to think that his name wouldn't come up at some point. But she wasn't prepared for the fact that he wasn't married. That he'd never gotten married. She'd always imagined him with a big family, living far enough away in Rome, where she had heard his fiancée was from.

She took another deep breath. At least now she would

be somewhat prepared. She didn't completely trust that Marco wouldn't tell Antonio that she was here, even though he'd promised her that he wouldn't. He'd have no reason to think it was such a big deal. The last Marco knew of their relationship, they were practically kids, hanging out, going on double dates together, without a care in the world. He didn't know about the secrets. Or the heartache Lia had caused. And now she'd have to deal with even more. She knew there would come a day that she'd have to tell Antonio everything. She just didn't want it to be so soon.

Lia tried to brush her new fears aside as she took the plates of pasta to her waiting guests in the restaurant. She'd cross the bridge when she needed to. There was no sense getting all worked up about it now. God knew, she didn't need to put poor Carlo through watching her angst again.

She left Rebecca and Marco to enjoy their meal; she went back to the kitchen to help Carlo clean up and start preparing for the dinner service, which would be happening before they knew it. Carlo had told her that the restaurant had been really busy, and she was happy for that. She knew that it was probably better for her mind to be focused on work, so she welcomed the distraction that it would bring. If she could just focus on the restaurant, maybe her pain would lessen. She knew that she'd never forget about Arianna or the memories. She didn't want that. She just knew that somehow her grieving—and hopefully her guilt——would lessen over time.

Rebecca called out to her in the kitchen that they were leaving. Lia went to give her friends a hug and thank them for coming.

"I'd love to get together. Maybe we could go for a walk or you could take a night off to grab dinner with me some time," Rebecca said, pulling her phone out of her handbag. "Let's exchange numbers anyway so that we can get a hold of one another."

Lia gave Rebecca her information and put her number into the new phone that she'd finally got around to purchasing a few days before. She felt skeptical about her new friendship now, if she was being honest with herself. But it wasn't fair to Rebecca or to her, really. Maybe they could maintain a friendship without Antonio's name coming up. Maybe one day she'd feel comfortable enough with Rebecca to tell her the story. Well, it was hard to imagine being able to share the whole story with her. Very few people actually knew it. But maybe this was to be part of the healing process for Lia. She'd remain open.

After Rebecca and Marco left, Lia told Carlo that she was going out for some fresh air after she made sure that everything was caught up in the kitchen. She really needed to clear her head and she thought a walk might help. She sighed, willing her anxiety to behave.

CHAPTER 14

The next few weeks passed quickly for Lia. She found herself developing a nice routine, spending most of her time in the restaurant. She still had her off days—even days where it was difficult to get out of bed—but she forced herself, and the effort seemed to be making a difference. At least it did from what people could see on the outside, she guessed, knowing that she still fought her inner demons every day.

She and Rebecca had developed a nice friendship, grabbing coffee or a short walk every few days or so. Lia really liked the bubbly woman and found that they seemed to have a few things in common. Rebecca was happy to be living in Tuscany and completely in love with Marco, but she also missed her family back in America.

The subject of Antonio hadn't come up again since the day in Thyme, and Lia was thankful for that. She could tell that Rebecca was someone she could trust; she found herself sharing more and more about her personal life, although nothing too uncomfortable had been shared yet.

Lia had finally agreed to take a night off from work to go to another of Rebecca's favorite restaurants in town. She supposed that it was important to check out the competition, and a night off would be good for her. Lia was waiting for Rebecca, who had agreed to pick her up at the inn, when there was a knock at her door. Elena had brought her guest upstairs. Lia suddenly found herself feeling slightly embarrassed, quickly tidying up the space that seemed perfect for her but suddenly seemed a bit small, as she'd never had a guest over before.

Elena left the two women, and Lia offered Rebecca one of the two seats in the little sitting area of the room. "Would you like a drink before we go?" Lia asked.

"No, I'm good, thanks," Rebecca said and Lia couldn't help but notice her expression as she glanced around the room.

"Okay, spill it." Lia laughed. "Go on, what are you thinking?" She was glad that their friendship had felt so easy so quickly. She couldn't help but be reminded of Gigi, and pushed back a sudden thought of missing her friend, back home, who already knew all of the sordid details of her life.

"Okay. I will," Rebecca said. "If you're insisting."

Lia nodded for her to continue.

"This place is lovely and everything. It really is. But how long have you been here now? Like a month?"

Lia nodded again. "Yes—and? Where are you going

with this?" She tried to lighten the mood with her laughter but Rebecca's face turned even more serious.

"Why haven't you found a place yet? What are you waiting for?"

"I don't know. I've just been busy, I guess. And if I'm honest, I've grown quite fond of Elena and Franco. I guess I'm comfortable here."

"Well, certainly finding a place to rent long-term—or buy, if that's what you're thinking of—would be more economical than staying here?"

Lia hadn't shared anything about her financial situation—the inheritance—with Rebecca. There'd been no reason to, and it wasn't a topic that one just brought up. Plus it brought with it so many questions that she knew she'd also have to answer, if she didn't want to leave the poor woman thinking she'd robbed a bank or something. She had shared with Rebecca already that she'd been working in San Francisco as a personal chef and housekeeper, so the fact that now she had loads of money wouldn't easily be explained away. Lia sighed, thinking about the best way to answer her questions.

"It's not the money. And yes, I do intend to buy a place. I'm just comfortable, I guess." Lia looked at Rebecca to gauge her next words. "And you're right. I should start looking. It is about time." She smiled, hoping that her friend would drop it for now.

"Okay, then. I happen to know someone. A lovely woman that helped Marco and me to find our place in

Greve. Can I call her? And maybe you'll let me set something up for you next week? I'll go with you if you like. I absolutely love looking at all the charming villas and apartments in the area." Rebecca grinned broadly, and Lia laughed in spite of the lurch she felt in her stomach at the thought of moving in somewhere.

"Yes, that would be fine and yes, I'd love for you to look with me. Now, let's go check out that other *favorite* restaurant of yours, shall we?"

"Oh, don't worry. Thyme will always be my favorite here. That happened even before I met you." Rebecca laughed as the two women got up to make their way to her car.

Lia thought the outside of the restaurant where they were going was lovely, and made a mental note that she might want to look into changing her table linen and the set-up of the outdoor patio at Thyme. The two women opted to dine outside in the nice evening air and settled in with a bottle of wine. Lia was feeling quite relaxed as the night went on and they shared easy conversation.

Rebecca shared with her that she'd met Marco just by chance: she was late for her cooking class one day because she had to have her favorite espresso from down the street where she'd been staying. They met while sipping their coffees at neighboring tables, and before she was finished, she'd agreed to hop on his motorbike for a tour of the wine country that she hadn't yet ventured to.

"And the rest—as they say, is history." Rebecca laughed. "Oh, and I never did make it back to that cooking class. I think Marco might just be regretting that to this day. Little did he know." She winked and Lia laughed, genuinely delighted to hear the story and be reminded of just how charming Marco had been when they were young.

Marco and Antonio had been inseparable back then, and she couldn't help but find herself wondering if they were still close.

"Penny for your thoughts." Rebecca was nudging her playfully across the table. "Hey, where'd you go just then?" They'd drunk nearly the whole bottle of wine, and Lia was feeling more comfortable than she'd been in a long time.

"Oh, sorry. What were you saying?" said Lia. "I love that story. Of how you and Marco met. He's a good guy. At least from what I remember." She smiled.

"He is. I adore him, really."

Lia watched Rebecca's whole face light up and wondered if it was the wine or simply the adoration of a newlywed for her beloved. Lia felt genuinely happy for her friend.

"So speaking of handsome Italian men…"

"Uh, I'm not sure that we were. Well, we were speaking of *your* handsome Italian man." Lia laughed, wondering where Rebecca was going with this, and instinctively feeling herself putting her boxing gloves on in defense.

"Well, Marco and I have this friend…"

"No, Rebecca." Lia laughed.

"He's so nice and very handsome, if I do say so—"

"Rebecca, please stop." Lia interrupted her, not meaning to sound quite as harsh as her voice did coming out of her mouth in response.

"Lia…"

Rebecca didn't look too bothered to Lia as she continued, either because of the wine or the fact that she was feeling comfortable enough with Lia now to know that she wasn't seriously offended by the conversation.

"No, Rebecca. I'm not ready to date. I really just want to be focused on the restaurant right now. And maybe finding a place to live," she added, hoping that she could successfully change the topic of conversation.

"It's just that—well, you're so lovely." Rebecca looked to Lia as if she was pouting, and Lia smiled in spite of her irritation, thinking that the look probably went a long way with Marco.

"Honestly, Rebecca. I've been through a lot." Lia sighed and she noticed the strange look on her friend's face, guessing that there was something else she wanted to say to her. "Rebecca? What is it?"

"God, you're going to be mad." Rebecca cringed as she said the words, taking a deep breath. "Marco did tell Antonio you were here. They were messing around—I think they'd both had plenty to drink—and Marco was telling him before I could stop him. I promise I tried to stop him."

Lia was a bit upset but she wasn't surprised. "Okay, and...?" she asked quietly.

"And, Antonio was so pleasantly surprised. I don't really understand why you didn't want him to know. He's absolutely gorgeous and delightful." Rebecca stopped for a moment, looking at Lia across the table. "He wants to see you. And I'm pretty sure he'll be coming into the restaurant soon." Rebecca rushed on, a concerned expression on her face as if worried about Lia's reaction to the news.

Lia sighed, running her fingers through her dark hair. There wasn't much to be done now except wait for it, she supposed. And she should be thankful to Rebecca for the heads up. She couldn't really fault her friend, and of course she'd be lying to herself if she didn't admit to being curious about Antonio. Especially after the way that Rebecca had just described him.

"So, when did this all happen?" Lia asked her friend.

"Just last night."

"And do you know where Antonio is staying?" Even hearing herself say his name out loud was causing her heart to pound so hard she thought surely everyone around her could hear it.

"He's staying near us at a little bed-and-breakfast at the moment. But he's actually in the final stages of buying a little winery near here. It's so beautiful. He gave us a tour the other day. I just know that you'd love it."

"Oh." Lia really needed to collect her thoughts. Suddenly she was feeling very overwhelmed and wasn't sure if the best thing for her was to be alone or finally have this big talk with her new best friend here.

Rebecca looked at Lia once more with an expression of worry. "Lia, I hope you're not too mad. I know Marco didn't really mean anything by it. I think he just knew that Antonio would want to see you—to know that you're here." She paused for a moment, seeming to take in Lia's expression before continuing. "Is it really that bad? No one's saying that you need to spend any real time with the guy, but if you were so close when you were young, why not at least take a minute to catch up with one another? I'm not sure exactly what happened between the two of you, but I'm sure enough time has passed to just let bygones be bygones. Don't you think?"

If only it were that simple. Lia thought to herself and made a decision that she hoped she wouldn't regret.

"Rebecca, are you in a hurry? Or do you have time for a nice long chat?" Lia winked.

"Oh, I've got all the time in the world." Rebecca settled back in her chair. "Shall we get another bottle then?" She smiled.

"Yes, I think I'm going to need it." Lia laughed, feeling more at ease with her new friend than she'd felt since she arrived in Tuscany.

The two women shared the remaining bottle of wine

as Lia proceeded to tell Rebecca the whole story of what had happened since the last time she'd seen Antonio so long ago. They talked for hours—well, mostly Lia talked, and Rebecca was an amazing listener, hardly containing her own emotions as they both wept when Lia told her about Arianna and the death that was such a shock to her.

When she was finished, Lia sat back, wiping her eyes and her nose one last time and taking a big drink of the wine remaining in her glass. She felt somehow lighter. It had been a good decision—sharing this all with her friend. She didn't know if it'd been the wine, her tears, or the act of actually retelling the story, but she felt as if a weight had been lifted from her shoulders. In the back of her mind, it did occur to her that she was going to have to retell this all to Antonio—that was really what counted. But she'd not shared the whole story with someone in a very long time and it felt surprisingly good to get it out. She looked over at Rebecca, who actually looked very drained herself.

She smiled at her friend. "Thank you for that. For listening. I guess I needed it."

"I don't know what to say. I'm so incredibly sorry for your loss. I can't even imagine everything that you've been through. To even begin to understand." Rebecca looked at her friend and continued. "And of course I get it now. Your reluctance to speak to Antonio. It's a lot."

"It is." Lia said in agreement, suddenly feeling very sleepy. "I feel better now, though, for sharing it with you.

I guess I feel that it's all going to have to be said to Antonio. Sooner, rather than later, and I just know that it's going to hurt him so deeply. That's the part I care about. Not necessarily the fact that he'll be angry and not want anything to do with me. That I can deal with. But I just—I never wanted to hurt him. Even back then, when we were kids—when I made the choices I made. Does that make sense?"

"It does. Yes," Rebecca said quietly.

Enough time had passed, enough sipping big bottles of water, that Rebecca would be sober enough to drive, and now the two were both practically falling asleep as they tried to chat about easier topics.

It had been a good night, and Lia was very thankful for her new friend here in Italy. How lucky she'd been when she chose that seat on the airplane next to her. The two women hugged, Rebecca assuring her that she was fine to make the thirty-minute drive home. And Lia promised Rebecca that she would keep her posted as to what happened when and if Antonio did come into the restaurant. They both knew that it was just a matter of time; and as Rebecca had said that she suspected by his reaction the other day, it would be sooner rather than later.

After saying goodnight to her friend, Lia made her way into the quiet house, stopping in the kitchen to get a bottle of water, surprised to fine Elena up at the stove making some warm milk.

"Can't sleep?" Lia said, trying to be careful not to startle her friend.

"Ah, bella. Did you have a good night with your friend? Rebecca was her name, *sì*?"

"*Sì*, we had a very good night." She smiled.

"Would you like a cup of warm milk? I've got enough here for two," Elena said, already getting another mug out of the cupboard as she spoke.

"Sure, *grazie*. Maybe I could use some help getting to sleep tonight." Lia saw the quizzical expression on her friend's face. "A lot on my mind." She pointed to her head and laughed.

"Ah, this will help then," Elena said, handing her the warm mug. "Sleep well. I will see you in the morning."

"Goodnight, Elena."

PAULA KAY

CHAPTER 15

The next day, Lia was in the kitchen at the restaurant, busy finishing up after the lunch service when Sofia burst in the door.

"Lia, someone's here to see you." Lia looked up to see her grinning at her as she spoke. "It's a man, and he's *very* handsome."

Lia's heart skipped a beat and she instantly felt panicked. It had to be Antonio. She thought she was prepared to see him, but now that he could possibly be standing right in front of her, she knew that she wasn't ready at all. God, maybe she should tell Sofia to tell him that she'd stepped out. She glanced out the doorway to see if she could catch a glimpse of him. There was a tall man with his back to the kitchen. Even without seeing his face, she knew it had to be him.

"Okay, thank you. Please tell him that I will be out in a minute and sit him at one of the tables—towards the back of the restaurant." She suddenly felt that maybe the best thing would be to blurt it all out and be done with it, and she didn't want to take the chance of having an audience when she did so.

She took off her apron and told Carlo that she would be back to help in a little while. She quickly went into their small bathroom to check herself in the mirror. Smoothing her dark hair, she tried to feed courage into the eyes staring back at her. *You can do this. He deserves to know everything and then it can be over. Don't think about it. Just tell him you have something to say that he is not going to like.* She took another deep breath and walked out into the restaurant.

Just as she was making her way across the floor to where he sat, he turned towards her, standing up to cross the short distance that separated them. Lia felt her heart beating wildly in her chest. *God, he was so handsome.*

"Lia, I can't believe it." He was kissing her on each cheek before she even had a moment to step away. "It's really you."

She swore that she could feel his eyes taking in her entire body as he spoke. And it shocked her, this visceral reaction she was having to being so near him. "Antonio, hello." She tried to smile, hoping that her face was responding in some way that wouldn't let him know how very nervous she felt. "It's good to see you too." And she meant it. Even though she had been dreading this moment, it was as if the past years had just vanished and she was a young schoolgirl standing in front of the boy that she loved.

"The years have been good to you," Antonio was

saying, still staring at her very intently. "Bella, you look wonderful."

Lia felt her face growing hot, and it shocked her that he was having this effect on her after all these years. "Let's sit." Lia motioned to Sofia, who was across the room watching the couple. "Sofia, would you get us a glass of the Chianti, please?" She tried to look at Antonio without blushing any more than she already seemed to be. "Is that okay for you?"

"*Sì*, anything is good." He reached for her hand across the table, his touch startling her in her chair. "I see that I can still make you blush." He laughed, as did she, despite her discomfort. "I have been looking forward to this moment ever since Marco told me that you were here. Is it true then? That you are here to stay?"

Lia thought he sounded like a little boy asking for something that he wanted to believe but just wasn't quite sure in the possibility. If she was being honest with herself, his obvious interest in her was catching her off guard. It had been a long time since a man had looked at her the way that Antonio was right now. He seemed genuinely very happy to see her, and she knew that any big secrets would not be revealed to him today. She'd enjoy the moment, even if it was all that they'd ever have.

"It's true. Yes," Lia said, wondering how little she could actually get away with *not* telling him right now. "The restaurant is mine—well, Carlo is still helping me to run everything, but I'm the official new owner of the place." She couldn't help but smile as she delivered the news, memories flashing that she'd long forgotten.

As if reading her mind, Antonio reached out to tuck a strand of hair behind her ear, whispering in a voice that Lia remembered all too well. "It was always your dream, bella. To cook. To have a restaurant. I am not surprised to see it has happened. I am only surprised that time finds us both here together now."

Lia was overcome by emotion. If it had been just any Italian man sitting in front of her, holding her hand and touching her hair, she would have been skeptical to say the least. But it was different with Antonio, and after one touch from him she was well aware of the genuine attraction between them. There had been real feelings of love all those years ago. She had never doubted it, and the intensity of their encounter now only strengthened all that she had once felt for this boy—man now—sitting before her.

She carefully took her hand away from his, trying not to make it too obvious but guessing that he could sense her discomfort. "It's strange after all this time. Seeing you. I've imagined it, but that was so long ago." She surprised herself with the honestly of what she was revealing, wondering if she could take it back. If she could easily send him away now. She doubted her resolve would hold for long.

"It is not strange to me." He winked at her. "It is how I imagined it many times." He reached for her hand again, his persistence testing her resolve. "When can I see you? Away from work?"

Lia couldn't seem to find the words to reply to his innocent question. She'd make a plan with him and then tell him everything the very next time she saw him.

Antonio was speaking to her again, and she had to ask him to repeat himself, as she was lost in her own panicked thoughts. "Can I see you tonight? Or tomorrow? In the morning? As soon as possible." He laughed, and Lia couldn't help but to join in at his silliness. "The time cannot come fast enough for me. We have so much to catch up on."

Lia took a deep breath, hoping that it was at least a bit discreet. "How about tomorrow morning? At the cafe just down the street. We can have a coffee before I come in to work."

"*Sì,* I will meet you there at ten o'clock. And I will count the minutes until then."

God, had he always been such a charmer. But she was enjoying his teasing looks and conversation. "Yes, that sounds lovely. I will look forward to it also." But inside she knew that she'd be terrified and dreading every minute because of the conversation that she needed to have with him.

They both stood and he pulled her to him in a big hug. Her body relaxed against his chest and once again she was shocked at the ease of being near him. They said goodbye, and Lia walked back into the kitchen feeling a little dazed.

Within minutes, Sofia was beside her, full of questions and grinning widely. Lia shooed her out of the kitchen, laughing and telling her to get back to work. That they'd talk later. She really needed a minute to collect her thoughts. She'd speak with Carlo about taking the night off, and she definitely needed to have a conversation with Rebecca. She had a feeling that Rebecca might be well aware that Antonio had planned to see her, and she'd be wondering about the outcome.

She finished a few other things in the kitchen and then took off for the rest of the night, calling Rebecca as she walked the few short blocks back to the inn.

The conversation was not surprising to her new friend. Yes, she'd known just that morning of Antonio's plans to see her, and was dying to know how everything had gone. Lia filled her in on their coffee plan for the next day, adding that she fully intended to tell him everything, and then that would be the end of it. Even as she was speaking to Rebecca, her heart sunk. She knew that when she told him, it was going to be bad. It would be over before anything ever even had a chance to start— and she thought that she was pretty clearly reading obvious signs of interest from him during their very brief meeting today. That would change, though. She sighed. She was sure of it. And better to do it sooner rather than later, or there would be even more for him to cope with.

Lia hung up with Rebecca, vowing to herself to put all

thoughts of Antonio out of her head. There was no use wondering about him—about them. She just had to keep moving forward with her plan to be honest and to get it over with. She'd been carrying the secrets for too many years. A part of her suspected that telling Antonio about the past might just be one of those big pieces of the puzzle that she needed to fit to be able to move on in her own grief. And guilt, she thought. If she could ever have a day without feeling guilty, it would be worthy of the biggest celebration.

She walked back to the inn and decided not to mention anything to Elena or anyone there about Antonio. It was a small place, and she suspected that Elena and Franco would know of Antonio's family.

Dinner was quiet that night, and Lia excused herself straight after with the excuse of how tired she was after a long day at work. She was feeling pretty exhausted, more emotionally than anything else, but she knew a good night's sleep would do her some good. She wanted to get up early to be sure she had time for a nice walk before her meeting with Antonio. The fresh air always seemed to help her to collect her thoughts, and she had a lot to formulate in her head for this conversation. Even the thought of it, as she lay in her bed, was causing her stomach to knot, and a huge amount of fear threatened to overtake her. Maybe she'd cancel in the morning, but even as she had the thought before drifting off to sleep, she knew that it would be silly to do so. She didn't need to prolong the inevitable. She needed to just get it done. Like ripping off a band-aid.

CHAPTER 16

Lia did wake early the next day, feeling surprisingly rested and clearheaded as she made her way to the dining room for one cup of coffee before the morning walk she had promised herself the night before. The early morning was bright and had just a slight chill, perfect and just the way she preferred it for her walk, which had become somewhat of a habit for her as of lately.

Lia came home with a resolve about the conversation that she would have with Antonio that morning. She carefully dressed in jeans and a crisp white t-shirt and headed early to the cafe where they were meeting. She wanted to have a moment to sit and relax before Antonio got there.

As she walked up to the door of the cafe, her heart lurched. Antonio was already seated inside, waving to her with a big smile when he saw her. He rose to greet her with a kiss on each cheek. "*Buongiorno*, Lia. I could not wait to see you this morning."

Lia smiled, noting to herself how infectious his smile

and happy attitude were. She didn't remember him being quite so charming, but the years had been good to him, both with looks and his charming personality.

"Good morning, Antonio. It's good to see you." Lia meant it, and felt her resolve lessoning just a bit.

They ordered coffee, and before she knew it an hour had passed during their easy conversation. Lia looked at her watch. "I think I must get to work now. I don't want to leave Carlo on his own for the lunch preparation. It was good to catch up with you, Antonio." She smiled, but her stomach was in knots because she'd failed to tell him anything real about the last years of her life. Anything that really mattered.

"Can I see you again? Will you give me your phone number?" Antonio had pulled out his phone and was ready to input the data.

Lia gave him her number by reflex, then wondered why she had done so. She'd agree to see him one more time and that would be it. She would tell him the next time she saw him. And suddenly she was agreeing to the date.

They would meet tomorrow night at another restaurant down the street. Antonio hugged her goodbye and promised to phone her the next day to confirm the time for their dinner.

Lia left the cafe feeling confused by her emotions. Why was it so hard to put thoughts of Antonio out of her head? She'd played the scene of seeing him so many times before in her mind; the shock of how she actually felt when she was near him seemed to be breaking any resolve to end it before it even began. But she knew what she had to do.

All day at the restaurant, she found her thoughts turning to Antonio, and it was difficult to concentrate. A new sort of dread had overcome her; she felt her heart growing heavy again with where she found herself at this juncture in her life. With it came the same feelings of loss about Arianna, as if she were having to deal with it all all over again. Lia sighed and let herself fall into the depression that she knew so well by now. She tried to make it through the whole day at the restaurant, but when she saw Carlo looking at her intently she decided to take the rest of the day off.

Lia went back and forth the next day about her date with Antonio. She just wasn't feeling up to it. She couldn't do it. She wouldn't go. She'd have to just deal with it another day when she was feeling stronger.

She had gotten a phone call from Gigi that she and Douglas were going to stop by the day after tomorrow upon arriving in Italy. They were to travel for several weeks before they'd come back for the big party that Lia had planned. They were headed down south to visit Gigi's family, but they wanted to see Lia first and were anxious to hear how things were going.

Lia had booked them a night at the inn, and now she was feeling slightly overwhelmed about their arrival even though she was desperate to see Gigi and catch up with her friend. She missed her and she really wanted to try to pull herself together. There was a lot to be done, with Blu and Jemma arriving in a few weeks and the party that needed to be arranged.

Lia hated to stand Antonio up, but she hadn't gotten his phone number, and she made the decision that it was for the best. She'd deal with the fact that he'd probably turn up at the restaurant again later. When the time had reached twenty minutes past the agreed restaurant meeting, Lia's phone rang.

She took a deep breath as she clicked the phone to take the call.

"Hello. Antonio?" She knew that it was him.

"Lia, is everything okay? I thought maybe our communications got crossed. I'm at the restaurant now."

Lia's heart lurched in her chest as she inhaled deeply. God, why was she so nervous?

"Antonio, I'm sorry to do this to you but I can't make it."

"Is everything okay?"

He sounded genuinely concerned, which made her next words all the more difficult.

"I can't see you right now, Antonio. It's too hard for me. With the restaurant, with everything. There's just so much going on."

Even to her own ear, the words sounded ridiculous.

The phone was silent on the other end and Lia tried

to imagine his expression.

"I don't understand." He paused. "I thought we had such a good time yesterday morning. I was really looking forward to seeing you again."

"I know. Yes, yesterday was nice and easy and, well, there's a lot of things you don't know about me, Antonio." She couldn't take the words back now.

"Yes, it's why I want to spend more time with you." She could almost see the smile that she imagined on his face.

"I just can't, Antonio. Please understand. I have your number now, so maybe I can call you another time. We will do it again. I promise." *I have to*, she thought.

"Goodbye." She clicked the phone off without waiting for his reply.

God, she'd be lucky if he even gave her a chance after that call. She had been so rude he'd probably not want to see her at all. Maybe she'd blown the chance to even be able to talk to him again, and for a minute it was what she wanted. But she knew that was cowardly. Now that she and Antonio were physically in the same place she owed it to him to tell him about the past. About Arianna. It had to be done at some point. And soon.

PAULA KAY

CHAPTER 17

Lia and Carlo had become quite the team in the kitchen. She was feeling pretty focused and trying not to let her emotions get the better of her. She was both excited and slightly nervous, because Gigi and Douglas were arriving in the evening. She'd take the night off at the restaurant, and she and Elena had put together a fun menu for dinner. She heard her phone buzz from across the kitchen, her heart sinking but knowing she should check it in case it was Gigi.

As she suspected, it was another call from Antonio. He'd been calling her ever since their last short conversation on the phone. So far, she'd not gotten up the nerve to answer, but she knew that if she didn't, it was only a matter of time before he'd show up again at the restaurant—which probably wouldn't go well.

Lia sighed. She would have to address him sooner or later, and she did feel incredibly rude in the way she'd ended their last phone conversation. She'd not worry about it just now, with company coming and so much to do at the restaurant; it would just have to wait until a better time.

The afternoon passed uneventfully, and Lia said goodbye to Carlo and Sofia as she headed out the door early to be back at the inn in time to greet Gigi and Douglas. She could hardly believe that they were actually going to be there in a few hours. It seemed like only yesterday that Douglas had dropped her at the airport with promises to see her very soon. She thought about everything she had to fill them in on. She knew that she'd try to gloss over the bits about her not quite feeling great just yet, the sad days that still threatened to overtake her; but she had seemed to pull it together for the last week or so. Well, until Antonio had popped up in her life. *Briefly,* she thought.

She went back to the inn to join Elena in the kitchen; they prepared the pasta for the dinner and her guests' arrival. She was happy that they would be joining her at the inn, but she did think that Douglas might have something to say about the fact that she'd not bothered to find herself a house yet. Hopefully, her friends would be gentle with her. At least she had set a day aside next week to look at a few places, so it wouldn't be as if she was making no progress.

The doorbell rang and both women went out to greet the guests.

Gigi and Douglas looked a bit tired after their big flight, but her friends' faces seemed to light up when they saw her, making her very happy.

"I'm so glad that you two are here. How was your flight?"

"It was pretty good, in terms of how long flights go," said Douglas.

Gigi laughed. "He wouldn't know. He slept nearly the whole trip. I had to wake him up just as we were landing in Florence." She winked at Lia. "You know you've been putting in a lot of hours at work when you can sleep for a whole uncomfortable plane ride."

Lia laughed and hugged her friends while Franco grabbed their bags. Elena showed them to their room to freshen up, letting them know that dinner would be ready shortly and to come to the front patio for a glass of wine anytime.

Lia felt her worries slipping away just a bit, happy to see the familiar faces of her friends who were so dear.

Dinner was lovely. The only other guests had checked out that morning so it was only Lia, her friends, and their hosts. The banter was easy. Gigi and Douglas quickly got Lia up to speed with everything that had been happening at home, and also their exciting plans for the delayed honeymoon that they were now taking in Italy.

"I really can't wait to introduce Douglas to my whole family," said Gigi, smiling at her husband beside her. Only one of her four sisters had been able to make it to the wedding, so there was still a lot of family for Douglas to meet.

Lia smiled as she listened to her friends speak. Their

joy seemed so apparent and wonderful. She truly was so happy for the way things had turned out for them.

Gigi turned to Lia. "So, tell us everything. How are you doing here? How's the restaurant?"

Elena got up to start clearing the dishes. "We'll let you all chat for a bit."

Franco followed, filling his guests' wine glasses before leaving.

"Oh, no need, Elena. I can help you with that," Lia said.

"No, no. Don't be silly. Enjoy your friends. I insist."

Lia smiled, turning back to Gigi to answer her question.

"Things are good. Fine. The restaurant has been pretty busy and Carlo is really great."

Lia hoped that she sounded more normal to them than she was really feeling inside.

Douglas looked as if he was stopping himself from saying something.

"What is it, Douglas? I know that look." Lia laughed.

"Oh, well. I was just wondering about your home. I mean, the inn is really great and Elena and Franco seem delightful. But you are looking at places, aren't you?"

Lia thought he seemed a little worried, which was the last thing she wanted.

"Yes, I thought you might wonder about that. I've just been really busy. Well, you know how it is. And the location here is so good for me. I can walk to the restaurant in only minutes," said Lia.

"Do you want me to help you?" Douglas glanced at his wife. "Because I'm sure that we could extend our time here a few days so that I could help you find something."

Gigi nodded, reaching for Douglas's hand under the table.

"Yes, of course we can," Gigi said.

Lia really did have the best friends in the world. She smiled at them both. "No, don't be silly. I don't want you to change anything. I actually have an appointment with a real estate agent next week and my friend, Rebecca— you'll meet her at some point—has agreed to help me look. I'm sure I'll have something by the time you two are back here for the party. Hopefully something big enough for all of us," Lia said, imagining a house filled with laughter and the loud sounds of Jemma playing.

"Okay; well, that sounds good then. If you're sure you don't need my help," said Douglas.

"You're very sweet to offer." Lia glanced at Gigi, who was hiding a yawn behind her hand. "Oh dear, you're looking pretty tired. Why don't I let you two go get yourselves tucked in. We have time tomorrow morning to catch up still."

Gigi laughed, not hiding the next yawn to come. "I think I will have to agree with that idea, although I do want to have a nice big talk with you in the morning."

"That's a date. I've taken the morning off from the restaurant, so maybe we can go for a nice walk or something. And speaking of the restaurant, I thought maybe we could go there for lunch before you two take off for the day?"

"That sounds wonderful on all counts," Gigi said as they all began to get up from the table.

"Sleep well," Lia said, giving her friend a quick kiss on the cheek.

CHAPTER 18

The next morning, Lia and Gigi met in the dining room over a nice cup of coffee.

"Douglas has gone out for a bit to investigate some of his travel ideas at an agency Elena told him about. I'm not sure what that man has up his sleeve, but I've already warned him that I don't particularly love surprises." Gigi laughed.

"Yeah, but if those surprises are nice little romantic getaways, that'd be okay, I suppose?" Lia smiled because she noticed that her friend was blushing slightly.

"Oh, I suppose so." Gigi got up from the table. "Shall we go for that walk you were telling me about last night? I feel like we never really got to talk about what's been going on with you—"

"Well, everything—" Lia interrupted her friend.

"Not just about the restaurant," Gigi said. And then she smiled at Lia. "I want to know how *you're* doing."

Lia met her eyes and just nodded. "Okay, let's go then. I'll tell you everything."

And she had decided just then to tell Gigi about Antonio showing up in her life. She'd long since filled her friend in on most, if not all, of the details as they pertained to Antonio and their past so long ago. Gigi was well aware of the secrets she'd been keeping from him for far too long. Maybe her friend would have a good perspective on everything, or at least help to calm her anxieties a bit about what she still needed to do. Lia sighed and tried to get Antonio out of her mind as they made their way to the footpath at the park near the inn.

They'd been walking for a few minutes, when Lia just decided to blurt it out—everything that had happened with Antonio. She told Gigi about meeting Rebecca on the plane and the surprise meeting between herself and Marco after that.

"Wow, what are the chances of that?" Gigi said, glancing at Lia. "So, do you know if Marco did tell Antonio?"

"He did, which honestly I assumed that he would," said Lia. "I'd been mentally preparing myself ever since the day I made the connection that they were cousins— well, I thought that I'd been preparing myself."

"What happened? Have you seen him?" Gigi said.

"Yes." Lia could hardly believe it herself even as she was relaying this news to her friend. After all these years, it seemed nearly impossible that she and Antonio had seen each other. "I've seen him a few times, actually."

"Oh? Go on," said Gigi.

"The first time was when he came into the restaurant. Of course I knew that it could happen, so I felt somewhat prepared, but then I saw him and—well, it's all over now anyways, so none of that really matters."

Gigi stopped on the path where they were walking, reaching out her hand to Lia so that they were facing one another. "You saw him and...? What happened and what's over?"

Lia laughed even though there wasn't really anything funny about the conversation they were having. She was uncomfortable telling this to her friend, and she couldn't quite put her finger on why. "Well, it's just that I'd be lying if I said that I didn't feel something with him—or if it didn't feel like there was something still between us."

"Okay, and this is a bad thing, why?"

"Gigi, I haven't told him about Ari," Lia blurted out. "I know I need to, but the times we've been together have been so strange—in a good way, I mean. I guess if I'm being honest, I just wanted to enjoy it for a minute—the possibility, or...I don't know. It's not a possibility." She looked away before she continued. "I stood him up the last time we were supposed to meet, and I've not been taking any of his calls."

"Lia—"

Lia thought she detected something else in her friend's voice. "I *will* do it. I mean, I intend to call him and get together one more time. I know that I need to tell him about Ari—about everything. And then it will just be over." She tried to sound as matter-of-fact about it as she could, but there was nothing simple about the situation.

"Lia," Gigi started again, and this time she was looking her straight in the eyes with a fierce expression that Lia hadn't seen before. "What are you doing?"

Lia definitely sensed the frustration, if not a bit of anger, in her friend's voice as she continued.

"You're not really thinking of Ari, are you?"

That was it. The change in tone that Lia had detected. She and Gigi had grown close, but there were still pieces of Gigi's personality that she had yet to learn about, and she especially couldn't discount the time that Gigi had spent practically raising Arianna. There was a fierce loyalty there, and that was what she'd seen on her friend's face when she'd mentioned Ari's name.

"I mean, do you not think that it's dishonoring her memory that you've not even told her father that she existed? I get that it's hard, Lia, but you owe that to her." Gigi wiped at the tears that had formed in her eyes.

"I will do it. I said that I would." She didn't know exactly what to feel about Gigi's words, but there was a new unsettling forming in the pit of her stomach.

"It's not only that—telling him about Ari." Gigi's voice grew gentler as she continued. "It's what Ari would have wanted for *you.*"

This was a conversation that they'd had before— many times, actually. But something about it suddenly felt different to Lia. She tried to keep it together, but the tears were coming anyways. "I don't mean to dishonor her memory—it's the last thing I would want." Lia was sobbing now and Gigi pulled her towards her for a hug. They made their way over to the bench nearby and sat down, sitting in silence for several minutes as Lia's sobs lessened.

Finally Gigi spoke again. "I don't think you mean to. I don't. What I do think is that you're scared and overwhelmed and—and a bunch of things I can't really begin to imagine."

Lia felt herself growing a bit calmer as she tried to quiet the voices in her own head enough to focus on her friend's words.

"I know that it hasn't been easy for you. God, what you've been through—what we've all been through—but especially you. I know there is guilt there." Gigi seemed to be waiting for Lia to look her in the eyes before she continued.

"I'll tell you that you and your daughter were not so different. She had that guilt too. Watching her finally let go of all that—at the end. It was really the best gift that she could have given herself. And—what I do know—is that she wouldn't have wanted you to be living the way you are now, Lia."

Lia opened her mouth to speak, ready to defend all the strides that she'd made since she'd been back in Italy. "I have—"

"You haven't, Lia. You're still holding on to this idea

that you can't really be happy, that you need to mourn Ari and keep punishing yourself. But I'll tell you that *that* is something that would have made Ari so angry."

Lia looked at her friend, listening intently and, maybe for the first time, genuinely hearing her words about what Arianna truly wanted for her.

"Do you have any idea how happy she would have been at the thought of you and her father finally being together again after all these years? She knew how much you had loved him, how you'd looked when you told her about him. How you looked just now, actually, telling me about seeing him again after all these years."

"That's all true, but he——"

"You don't know. I'm sure he's going to be shocked and yes, probably angry. Anyone would be, but you can't just automatically discount everyone, Lia. Not everything has to turn out bad just because it's what you *think* you deserve." Gigi's voice grew quieter again. "Maybe you deserve something wonderful in your life."

The two women sat in silence for another minute.

"Arianna gave you all of this—the restaurant, the home you've not purchased yet, a new chapter of your life here in Italy—not because of anything that had to do with her wealth, but because she was trying to give you the redemption of your own dreams, of everything that you had once given up."

Both of the women were silently weeping as Gigi continued, speaking the truth about who Arianna was in a way that Lia had not *really* heard before.

"And Lia—if Antonio ends up being a part of that—and maybe he won't be—but you owe it to yourself—to Ari, to give that a try—to give all of this a *real* try."

Lia nodded to her friend, wiping the last of her tears away with her hand. She felt something shift inside her as they walked in silence back to the inn. Gigi had been right about everything. She *had* only been going through the motions with all of the changes, and it hadn't really gotten her anywhere. She felt a new resolve within her. She'd phone Antonio after Gigi and Douglas left. She'd meet him and tell him everything. Whatever happened after that, she'd be ready for.

Arianna had given her so much—wanted so much for her. It was time that she truly accepted the gift from her daughter—it was time that she started *really* living the life that Arianna had wanted for her.

PAULA KAY

CHAPTER 19

Lia stepped into the foyer of the small villa and couldn't contain a little shout of excitement as she looked over her shoulder at her friend Rebecca.

"This place is so sweet. Just like how I'd picture a quaint little villa," Lia said.

The two women followed the agent throughout the house, listening to her describe the centuries-old villa. It had been empty for the past year, but the owners had hired a service to keep up the grounds and the interior of the house.

There were three bedrooms of average size, and two and a half baths. Lia stepped into the kitchen, her eyes drawn to the large workspace in the center of the room and the sunlight that was streaming in through the big windows. On one side of the kitchen was a little nook, perfect for a small table, and windows that looked out onto the garden just outside.

"You look really happy in this kitchen," Rebecca said. "I think you may have just found the one."

Lia paused at the window, considering her friend's

exclamation. "I'm not so sure." She noticed Rebecca's quirked eyebrow. "I mean don't get me wrong, I love it and everything. I'm just thinking about the one we just saw, too."

"You mean the one with six bedrooms and the pool?" Rebecca asked.

They had looked at several different villas available in the area. Lia hadn't really given the agent a number in terms of her price range, so they had seen everything from very small, modest villas to huge towering mansions. Rebecca seemed a bit shocked that Lia would go for the other, and Lia felt the need to explain herself.

"I'm just thinking about next month, when everyone comes from back home to visit." *And what Arianna would have preferred*, she couldn't help thinking. "We'll need a lot of room and I want things to be perfect." *I want it to be like before, when Arianna was here too.*

"Okay, you know what you want. It's just that you really seem to light up in this place. I don't know. It's as if you belong here," Rebecca said. "I'm not sure that buying a huge place is the best idea if you are doing it just to accommodate guests that will visit once in awhile. I mean, there are plenty of places that you can rent for those occasions, right?"

"Oh, I know," Lia said. "It's just for some reason, I think the other one is the best choice for me." She turned to the agent to find out the prices for both of them, noticing Rebecca's face as they discussed the high price of the bigger home.

"Is the other home available for rent, by any chance?" Rebecca asked the agent.

"I'd have to make a phone call to the owners to find out for sure, but it is an option that they were open to at one time."

Lia nodded, thankful that her friend was with her; Rebecca seemed to have an idea of something that Lia was missing. "That's not a bad idea," she said, even though as she thought about Arianna, she knew it would be the home she'd end up in. *It's what she would have wanted for me.*

Lia and Rebecca left the villa, and the realtor promised to call Lia as soon as she'd spoken with the owner. The two women decided to stop off at a cafe nearby for a coffee and to end the nice day with a chat.

"Thanks so much for putting me in touch with the agent and for coming with me today. It means a lot. Way less daunting than doing it on my own," Lia said and laughed.

"Oh, no problem at all. It's fun for me. I never get tired of seeing all the villas and lovely homes here in the countryside. Half the time, I'm still pinching myself to wake up from this dream I think I'm having." The two women laughed.

"It's no dream." Lia smiled. "I'm really happy for you and Marco. You two seem very well suited for one another."

"Speaking of being well suited…" Rebecca started to say.

"Rebecca, don't start. Please." Lia tried to look stern, and calm her heart from racing—which seemed to always be the case whenever she thought about Antonio.

"Lia, you really need to phone him," Rebecca said gently. "He's been over a few times and he's tried to get information out of me. Quite frankly, it's making me a little bit uncomfortable, knowing what I know—"

"I know. I'm really sorry. I am."

Lia hated that she was putting her friend in this position. It really wasn't fair.

"Well, I just think it's not fair to him. I'm not judging you, but he deserves more of an explanation than what you've given him, if you ask me—and I realize that you are *not*," Rebecca said, laughing a bit nervously.

Lia liked this about Rebecca. Her honesty and straightforward approach was refreshing.

"You're right. You are," Lia said. "I'll call him."

"Really?"

"Yes, really. I'll do it tonight when I get home. He does deserve more than what I've told him. He deserves to know everything." *And then it can just be over*, she thought, at the same time wondering if she'd really have the courage to follow through with it.

The two women finished their coffee, and Rebecca dropped Lia off back at the guest house, with promises of phone calls and a get-together again soon. Lia had dinner

with Elena, Franco, and a few guests, retiring up to her
room with a big glass of wine. She needed the liquid
courage to make the phone call.

Antonio answered on the third ring. "Hello, Lia."

The sound of his voice made Lia sit in the chair that
she had been standing near. *God, he sounded so wonderful.*

"Antonio, hi." She couldn't help but smile as she said
his name, and she imagined the grin that was across his
own face as he replied to her.

"I've been so worried about you, bella. Are you okay?
Is there anything I can do?" Antonio said, and the
concern in his voice made Lia's heart pound even faster.
"Or is it that you just don't have any interest in seeing
me?"

She could almost imagine the expression on his face,
and for a brief moment all she could think about was
kissing his worries away. She shook her head as if
attempting to rid herself of the image.

"I know. I'm so sorry. I've been completely rude to
you," Lia blurted into the phone. "Yes, I'm okay, but—
Antonio, I do need to talk to you. To tell you everything."
There it was. There was no going back now. This was a
conversation that needed to happen.

"*Sì*, it's no problem. When can I see you?
Tomorrow?"

"Yes, tomorrow would be good. Maybe you can come
by here and we'll go for a walk in the park nearby?" She
didn't want to have this conversation in a public place. It

was too private, and she wanted to at least give Antonio the space to react in whichever way he needed to. She could at least grant him that.

"Sure. That sounds good. I will come by around ten o'clock?"

"Yes, ten is great," Lia said through the lump in her throat.

"And Lia," Antonio's voice was quiet and so sincere. "There's nothing that you can tell me that is going to change how I am feeling about you, how I'm feeling about this second chance that we have to get to know one another again."

"I'll see you tomorrow," Lia said as she clicked off the phone, tears streaming down her face. *I bet I can change your mind about me.*

CHAPTER 20

Lia sat in her room waiting for the sound of the doorbell. She was glad that she and Antonio would be staying nearby, and she had a chance to feel somewhat composed before she saw him, unlike all of the other times she'd seen him or heard his voice.

She took a deep breath when she heard the doorbell ring, and walked downstairs just in time to see Elena letting Antonio in. She made the introductions and Elena excused herself, leaving the two of them standing rather awkwardly inside the door.

Antonio reached to kiss her cheeks and then grabbed her in a very familiar embrace. *God, the smell of him.* She couldn't believe how easy her body slipped into his arms, how easy it would be to place her cheek against his broad chest, and just rest it there for a little while. She cleared her throat and willed herself to stop the thoughts that were threatening her motivation for this meeting.

"You look so beautiful." He was looking at her intently. "Thank you for calling me, for meeting with me."

"Thank you, Antonio. And for coming. I—I'm happy that you agreed to see me after the way I blew off our date the other night. I really do apologize for that."

"It's okay, bella. All that matters is that we are here now." Antonio reached for her hand, and Lia pulled it away as she moved towards the front door, trying not to look at his face while doing so.

"Shall we walk for a bit? There's a park with a nice footpath nearby. We can talk there." She hoped her voice didn't sound as odd as it did to her own ear. She was so nervous.

"*Sì*, that sounds nice. Can I take your hand now, please?" He winked at her, and she found herself laughing in spite of her admonition to herself to be serious.

She allowed him to take her hand. As they made their way to the park, they walked in easy silence, Lia lost in her own thoughts about how to start the conversation that she must have rehearsed in her head one hundred times. Antonio just looked happy.

She stole a glance at him as they walked along the path. He was the boy she had fallen in love with and more. So much more. If she allowed herself to think about it, the possibility of knowing him now, as a woman—she grew weak in the knees, and her heart, just thinking about it. He was every bit the type of man she or any woman would be lucky to have, and in moments the very idea of anything between them would be crushed.

Lia sighed, and it didn't go unnoticed by Antonio.

"What's wrong, Lia? You seem so sad. Do you not trust me?"

"No, it's not that. You've been lovely. Really." She pulled him over to a bench at the side of the path and they both sat down. She took a deep breath as he watched her intently.

"What is it?" He reached over to put a strand of hair behind her ear. "I promise you it's going to be okay."

She couldn't help the tears from falling as she tried to find the words that seemed impossible. "God, I really don't know how to tell you all this." She looked at him and willed him to tell her to "never mind". But she knew better, and only had to do what she knew was right.

"Lia, just tell me." He reached for her hand, holding it gently in his lap.

Lia took a deep breath. "When I left you here in Italy for America…all those years ago…Antonio, I found out that I was pregnant." She looked at him then, seeing the first glimpse of shock across his face.

"What?"

"I had a baby girl—Arianna." She didn't want to stop and think about it now. She had to keep going with the information. "I—we had a daughter." She looked at him, tears streaming down her face.

"Where is she is?"

She couldn't quite read Antonio's face but she guessed that he was still feeling the shock of it.

"Antonio, she——I——" She looked up at him, willing herself to continue. "I don't know how to tell you this."

She felt Antonio's body stiffen next to her as he dropped her hand. "Tell me what, Lia? Where is my daughter? This is a lot to——to take in." He looked at her with pleading eyes. "I want to know about her."

"Antonio, she——she died last year." Lia looked down at her hands, quietly sobbing and unable to look at the man beside her.

Antonio was on his feet and she could sense his confusion, his anger. He ran his fingers through his hair, looking like he didn't quite know what to do with his hands.

"I——I don't know what to say. God, Lia."

Lia sat in the stillness for a minute looking down at her hands sobbing. She could feel him waiting for her to look up, to acknowledge his confusion. She raised her face to meet his eyes and the pain she saw there was like a punch to her gut.

"Antonio, I'm sorry. I'm just so sorry." She stood to reach out to him and he pushed her hand away, taking a step back.

He sat back down on the bench and she sat next to him. He looked at her then. "Tell me everything. I really don't understand any of this."

They sat there for quite some time as Lia filled him in on all the details, trying her best to answer all of his many questions.——Lia crying throughout most of it and Antonio barely containing the anger that she felt sure was right there at the surface of his confusion. And she didn't blame him at all for it. She knew that he'd be dealing with so many different emotions, and that it would all take a long time for him to process. She had prepared herself for that and guessed that there would be more questions to come.

Antonio stood up. "I need to go now." He didn't ask her to follow him and Lia didn't make a move to get up off the bench. His face was stern as he looked off into the distance, barely able to look at her. It was what she'd expected. She wasn't surprised.

"I'm sorry, Antonio. For everything." Her words sounded so silly, even to her own ears.

There was no way to really convey the depth of her feelings. All she could do was move forward, and at least she no longer had the burden of knowing that it was a secret kept from Arianna's father. Finally, he knew the truth; and maybe eventually she'd be able to share all of the wonderful things about his daughter with him. He deserved that. For now, she just watched him walk away, as she sobbed alone on the bench.

PAULA KAY

CHAPTER 21

Lia stepped back to admire the pictures she'd placed on the mantel, wondering if she would ever have more things to make the giant space feel lived in. God knows she didn't really think that she needed more things. *Just people and laughter*, she thought.

"I love the pictures," Rebecca said, stepping up to take a closer look. I feel like I know them all already." She reached for the picture of Arianna. "She's so gorgeous."

"That was taken when we were together in Italy. In Florence." Lia remembered the day so clearly. They'd been out shopping in the market and Lia had snapped the shot of Arianna, looking so happy and carefree in the late morning sunlight, her thick, dark hair wild and loose around her face.

She turned to Rebecca as her friend set the picture back down with care. "Yes, she was beautiful, inside and out. I wish that you could have met her," Lia said.

"I wish that too." Rebecca gave her quick hug and then took a survey of the empty boxes sitting around them in the big living room. "I think that's the last of it, yes?"

Douglas had hired a service to ship all of Lia's things to her; the week prior to moving into the villa had gone quickly as Lia, with Rebecca's help, purchased the items she would need to settle in. She'd ordered a lot of beautiful things from shops in Rome, and still had to put the finishing touches on the bedrooms that would be used by her guests in just a few weeks time.

She felt tired and a bit out of sorts as she looked around the big villa the owner had decided to rent to her month-to-month. It had taken some doing and a hefty price, but she was happy that it was done for now. She felt she'd get used to the size of it. It just all seemed so strange and foreign to her right then.

"Thanks so much for your help. I could never have done all this without you." She hugged Rebecca, feeling so grateful for their friendship. "I'd love to have you and Marco over for dinner soon."

"That would be great. We will never pass up your delicious cooking," Rebecca said, sitting down on the sofa and putting her feet up. "I say it's time for a little break."

"Good idea. I'll get us a glass of wine." Lia busied herself in the kitchen, thinking about the big elephant that had been in the room all morning—well, really it had been for the past weeks now, ever since she had filled Rebecca in on what had happened between her and Antonio. She had guessed that Rebecca didn't want to be involved in it—or more correctly that there wasn't anything positive to say, so she had nothing she wanted to relay to Lia. And Lia understood that. But she couldn't help but wonder about him, no matter how hard she tried to banish him from her mind.

She set their glasses down on the table in front of the sofa, taking a seat herself.

"So, how is Antonio?" Lia said.

Rebecca eyed her carefully before speaking. "I thought this was a topic that you didn't want to talk about?"

"True. But I can't help it. I mean, I know he's got to be incredibly hurt and angry with me. I just wonder how he's doing—if you know how he's doing?"

"I honestly don't know a lot. The last time he was over, I heard him talking to Marco and yes, he seemed very upset. I'm not going to lie to you about that."

Lia nodded for her to continue.

"But you knew that was coming," Rebecca said.

"Yes, I did." Lia couldn't keep the tears from starting. She had been going through the motions the past few weeks—making decisions about her move, working in the restaurant, trying to just get on with her life. But Antonio was never far from her thoughts. She didn't know if she would ever *not* think about him and how he was doing. Reconnecting with him in Italy had done that to her: rekindled feelings that she'd never dared to revisit before.

"Maybe he just needs time," Rebecca said quietly. "I can tell you that his purchase of the vineyard was finalized. I'm sure he's been keeping busy with all there is to do with that. You never know," Rebecca said.

"I'm not holding out any hope for the two of us. I just hope that one day I can share more about Ari—about his daughter—with him. Show him her pictures, the music that she loved, the memories that I do have of her." At this Lia felt intense guilt. Memories that she'd not given him the chance to have with her. If only she'd tried to make that happen a year ago, maybe then things could be different. Except they wouldn't be. Not really. Arianna would still be gone.

"Well, I still think he just needs some time. He might come around." Rebecca reached over to hug her friend. "You've done the best you could with a really difficult situation. I think you are handling it all pretty well."

Lia sighed. "Well, I'm not really sure how else to handle it, except maybe to have a nervous breakdown." She laughed lightly. "And I don't think that would be pleasant for anyone, so I'll just keep going forward."

Rebecca nodded in solidarity.

"I have enough to focus on right now, with the restaurant and everyone coming in just a few weeks. I really can't wait to introduce you to Gigi and Blu. Of course, I'd love to have you and Marco come to the party. I'm sure that you all will fit right in with this little family of mine.

"That sounds really nice," Rebecca said. "We'll look forward to it."

CHAPTER 22

Lia kept herself busy over the next few days. Between cooking in the restaurant and working to get the villa ready, she had more than enough to keep her mind occupied—except her thoughts did continually turn to Antonio, much more than she would have liked.

One day as she was busy cleaning up after the lunch service, Sofia stopped her in the kitchen.

"Lia, Antonio is here to see you."

Lia's heart pounded as she slipped into the restroom to check her hair in the mirror. She took a few deep breaths, mentally preparing herself for what she knew could be another difficult conversation. She walked out into the restaurant and Antonio was beside her within seconds, crossing the room to embrace her the moment she was in his sight.

She let herself sink against his chest, feeling the strength and his forgiveness all at once. She brought her head back to look him in the eye. "Antonio?"

He smiled at her and pulled her close again,

whispering into her ear. "I've been so lost these past couple of weeks, bella. I've been so angry and confused."

She looked down and knew her tears were coming.

He placed a finger under her chin, tilting her face up, forcing her to look him in the eye. "But I also know that I want you in my life. I want to know more about Arianna—I want to get past the hurt and anger. I think I can do that if you'll allow me—allow us—a chance?"

Lia looked into his eyes and felt shocked. She almost couldn't believe that it was happening. She didn't deserve it. That much she knew was true.

"I—I don't know what to say. How can you possibly forgive me? It's not something I would ever ask or expect of you, even though I want it so desperately."

He reached out to wipe her tears away with his finger. "I'm not sure how things will turn out. I can't promise you anything about the future right now. I just know that I've been a wreck these past two weeks. And I think that spending time with you will somehow help me to see clearly. Does that make sense?"

Lia nodded her head before placing it against Antonio's chest again. "It's more than I could ever hope for."

He held her tight for a moment and she could feel his heart beating. She looked up at him. "I want to tell you everything about Ari. She was special and you would have adored her, Antonio." She saw the tears threatening in his eyes as he took a deep breath.

"I'd like that, starting with pictures. I want to see what she looked like—our daughter." He quickly wiped the single tear away across his cheek. "I picture her looking just like you." He smiled at her then.

"Oh, she was much more beautiful than I was at her age." Lia could feel herself blushing. "I've moved from the guest house."

"I know." Antonio smiled. "Rebecca told me about the villa. Or I should say that she warned me about the massive size of it?" He laughed.

"Would you like to come by? Maybe tomorrow for lunch? I'm sure Carlo will be fine without me for the day." She could hardly believe this was happening. "Just to talk and to look at pictures."

'*Sì*, yes, I'd like that very much." His mouth grew a bit sterner. "I don't know exactly what will happen. I can't make promises, but I am willing to take it one day at a time if you are."

"Yes, thank you."

Lia brought the photo album of Arianna over to the couch where Antonio sat waiting, an expectant look on his face. She still couldn't believe that he was there with her now. She'd been in a happy daze ever since leaving the restaurant the day before. Looking at him now, sitting here in the villa with her, was more than she ever could have dared to imagine.

She opened the book to one of the first pictures that

she had taken of Arianna, the day that they'd arrived in Florence, her dark hair framing a face with little make-up and the wide grin that Lia had come to love so much.

Antonio brought the book closer to him to peer intently at this woman who had been his daughter. "She's so beautiful." His voice caught a bit and Lia could sense the magnitude of emotion as he turned each page, peering at the pictures. "She does look like you, bella." He smiled, taking Lia's hand.

"She has your nose, I think," Lia said. "She was so lovely, Antonio." It was hard not to cry talking about her now, with him. And Lia didn't hold back her tears.

As Antonio flipped through the pictures of Arianna in Tuscany, including the ones with Carlo and Sofia at the restaurant, he grew quiet and Lia could feel his body tensing just a bit. "I can't believe that she was here—that you both were here not so very long ago. I was in Rome then. But I—I would have come, Lia. I so would have liked to meet my daughter."

Antonio wasn't shy about the tears that had formed in his eyes; Lia looked at him, hoping that he really knew the depth of her sorrow over the mistakes that she'd made. "I'm so sorry. I wish so much that I could go back in time. For you, but for Arianna too. It's a mistake that I will always feel guilty for, and I hope that one day you can forgive me."

Antonio wiped at his eyes and pulled Lia in for a hug, stroking her hair and whispering to her. "I know, bella. I know you're sorry. And I do forgive you." He looked at her then. "If we have any chance of seeing if something can work between us, you have to know that."

Lia nodded, trying her best to fully understand the scope of what he was telling her. She had barely allowed herself to think that she could have the second chance that she'd gotten with Arianna. Having it with Antonio as well was unbelievable to her. She didn't want to mess this up. She felt that she owed it to Arianna to try to really give this a shot. She smiled as she thought about what Ari would have said about the fact that Lia was sitting there holding hands with her father, the love of Lia's life that she'd told her daughter about.

"What's so funny?" Antonio asked with a grin.

"Oh, I was just thinking how pleased Ari would have been that I was sitting here with you right now." She looked up at him, suddenly feeling a little shy. "I did tell her about you, you know. I told her that you were the love of my life." She smiled, wondering if Antonio could feel the quickening of her heartbeat. She hadn't really been this close to him, in proximity or emotionally, since the two had reconnected in Italy.

Antonio looked her intently in her eyes and reached for her chin, tilting her face slightly as his lips brushed hers, deepening into that first kiss she'd been waiting for, yet not dared to imagine.

Her whole body felt the shock of his kiss. It was as if the years melted away and they were the two young kids taking advantage of the few minutes alone on a sofa before their parents walked in. It was all they could do to pull themselves away from one another when Lia got up to get them a glass of wine.

"I can't believe what you are doing to me, bella," Antonio laughed. "After all these years. It's crazy."

Lia handed him the glass of wine, smiling. "Crazy good? Or crazy 'what the hell am I doing?'" She laughed.

Antonio laughed too as he lifted his glass of wine for a toast. "Crazy good." He leaned over for a quick brush of her lips. "To Arianna—to my daughter."

They clinked their glasses together. "And to you, bella." He kissed her again.

Lia kissed him back and then pulled away. "Wow. I really can't believe any of this." She laughed. "Do you think we should slow down a bit?"

He looked at her intently and she wondered what he was thinking.

"Yes, I think that you are right. As much as I'd like to pick you up and carry you to that lovely bedroom you showed me on the tour…" He laughed.

Lia's heart quickened, and she couldn't help the image that raced through her mind. It had been so long since a man had looked at her with such longing. She'd forgotten what it felt like to feel wanted like that. And she did want him. They had to go slower, though. Too much had happened. She couldn't bear for things to end badly with them if it didn't work out; and she did know from experience that intimacy could get in the way of any type of reason when it came to relationships. For now, they'd take the time to get to know one another.

"What is this music, by the way?" Antonio said, interrupting her thoughts.

"It's *La Bohème*."

"Ah, so do you like opera?"

Lia waited a few seconds before answering, wondering if it was odd that she had to think about such a question. "I never really did, no. But it—it was Ari's favorite. It reminds me of her so much." Antonio nodded as if he understood exactly everything that was said in that short sentence.

Lia went on to tell him about going to the opera with Arianna and how the young woman loved to drive her convertible through the city, with the top down and opera music blaring. She was so thankful that she'd had those memories with her—with their daughter—to recount to him now.

They spent an easy couple of hours together, Lia serving them a nice salad out in the garden for lunch before Antonio had to be on his way. They made plans to talk soon and arrange their first official date. Lia was incredibly happy as she kissed him goodbye, hardly believing her good fortune, and willing herself to just be in the moment, something that she had learned from her time with her daughter.

PAULA KAY

CHAPTER 23

Lia came out of the dressing room to show Rebecca the very fashionable long red gown that was one of several she'd picked out as a possible purchase for the opera. She had told Antonio that she was planning a surprise weekend for him; she'd booked two nights at the Four Seasons in Florence and purchased opera tickets for *La Boheme*.

She knew that it would be bittersweet, being back in the luxurious hotel where she'd last stayed with Arianna, but ever since she'd shared her daughter's pictures and that first kiss with Antonio, she had pledged to herself and to her daughter that she was committed now, determined to set aside her grief and guilt and live the life that Arianna would have wanted for her. Her big villa, the opera tickets, the reservation in Florence, and even this fancy dress were all things that Arianna would have wanted her to have, and she was trying her best to honor her daughter and all that she had left her.

"What do you think?" Lia asked Rebecca as she gave a little twirl.

Rebecca hesitated, eyeing her thoughtfully. "It's nice."

"But?" Lia laughed. "You don't think it's a good color on me?"

"No, it's not that. The dress is lovely. And you look gorgeous as always." Rebecca smiled. "It's just—I don't know. I'm not used to seeing you so dressed up. And it's a lot to spend on a dress, yes?"

Lia looked down to glance at the price tag. "It is. You're right. But it just feels like I need something special for the occasion. I want everything to be perfect for the weekend, for Antonio." She felt her face blushing.

"Are you talking about what I think you're talking about?" Rebecca teased. "Are you saying that the two of you haven't slept together yet?"

"Well, no. We haven't. Well, not as adults, anyways. We've been taking it slow. And quite frankly, I don't know that anything will happen during our time away, either. Antonio has gotten pretty old-fashioned with his thinking and I—well, I think it's refreshing, really." She could definitely feel her face growing hot. She and Rebecca had grown very close but they hadn't had a lot of discussion when it came to such intimate details of their lives.

"Well, I think that's nice," Rebecca said. "You and Antonio have waited a long time to be together. There's no reason to think that you might not be getting your fairy-tale ending." She winked at her friend. "And honestly, when he sees you in that dress—which I think you have to have—I'm not sure that he's going to make it through the weekend sleeping apart."

Lia laughed as she turned to go back into the dressing room. "Well, I did book us separate suites, so that's not really my agenda." She turned back to wink. "I just thought it would be fun to take him away and share the opera with him. Something that Ari had shared with me. Does that make sense?"

"It does."

Lia couldn't quite put her finger on what she was detecting in her friend's voice today, but Rebecca seemed to be biting her tongue about something. She tried to put it to the back of her mind as she got dressed, excited to purchase the gown and take her friend out to a restaurant that she'd heard a lot about. They had flown down to Rome for the night, and Lia was enjoying treating Rebecca to a few things for all of the support that she'd given her. She had tried to get her to try on a few dresses herself, but she'd insisted that it wasn't her style at all and she had no place to wear anything quite so fancy.

The two women enjoyed a delicious lunch of fresh pasta and a lovely bottle of the nicest wine. The conversation with Rebecca was easy, and Lia tried to put her earlier thoughts out of her mind. She had only been to Rome a few times since she'd been back, and she enjoyed the city even though she much preferred her quiet life in Castellina. It was hard to imagine Antonio here though, working in the city, wearing a suit and tie. He seemed so at home in his new vineyard, and it reminded Lia of the young man she'd fallen in love with, tanned skin from working out in the fields, calluses on his fingertips.

They had been spending quite a bit of time together ever since their kiss that morning at Lia's. Mostly it had been good. They'd been for a few walks and enjoyed several coffees and meals at the local restaurants around town. But if she was being honest with herself, something seemed to be not quite right. She couldn't put her finger on it, and she was trying so hard with him. She wondered if it would help to talk to Rebecca about it and decided that she had nothing to lose.

"Penny for your thoughts." Rebecca was laughing, snapping her fingers in front of Lia's face.

"Oh, sorry. I guess I have a lot on my mind."

"Yeah, where were you just now?" Rebecca teased.

"I was just thinking about Antonio. About the last dinner that we shared together."

"And...? What about it? Happy thoughts?" Rebecca winked.

"Well, no—not exactly. I can't quite put my finger on it and I almost don't want to say it out loud. Something just feels kind of awkward. I'm really trying, though. So hard. And I think he is too." She sighed.

"Well, maybe you just need to give it some time. I mean, you did hit him with a lot of information. I'm sure it's a lot to process along with a new relationship. Time will tell. Just be your lovely self," Rebecca said.

That's what I'm afraid of. That I won't be good enough. That he will see all of this ugly guilt and shame inside of me. Lia couldn't seem to squash the thoughts that were always in her head, no matter how much she tried to push them aside, to stay focused on seeing Arianna's face and her words instead.

Lia felt great being back full-time at the restaurant—almost like herself again. And for the first time in a long time, she felt hopeful. She still had her moments, feeling a lot of grief about Arianna and the mistakes of the past, but she'd really been trying to commit to her new life here, a life that included Antonio. She knew that would be honoring to Arianna, that it would have made her daughter happy, and she was trying her best to respect her wishes.

"Lia." Sofia popped her head in the kitchen. "Antonio is here for you."

"Thanks. Tell him I'll be right out." Lia went to the restroom to check her hair, feeling her heart race just a bit as it often did when she thought about Antonio.

He rose to embrace her and give her a warm kiss on the lips, which Lia reciprocated with ease. Sofia let them know that Carlo was preparing lunch for them; she served them a glass of wine to sip while they waited.

"How are you, my darling?" Antonio said, reaching for her hand across the small table.

Lia felt her smile broaden. "I'm well, thank you. And

you? How is everything at the vineyard today?" She had only been to his new place a few times and was already in love with the property. She could see the draw to the lifestyle, and Antonio seemed perfectly at home there.

"Oh, good. You know, lots to do."

"Are you looking forward to a little time away this weekend?" Lia could feel her face growing slightly warm at the mere thought of spending an entire weekend away with this handsome man sitting in front of her.

"I'm looking forward to spending time with you, bella." Antonio winked. "But I do wish you'd let me in on what the big surprise is. The fact that you've told me I need a tux is making me a bit uneasy." He laughed. "I don't really have much occasion to dress so fancy these days, you know."

"I know. But it will be nice. Trust me." Lia studied him carefully for a moment. "Shall I order you a tux? I'm certainly happy to do so."

"Oh, no. I do have one. Don't worry about that."

Lia knew that it was probably the tux he'd purchased for his wedding that never happened. They really hadn't discussed his previous relationship. There were so many hurdles to get over, balancing the many conversations that they still had to wade through, that she wondered how much it even mattered. But of course it did, and it should be talked about.

"Is it—was it the tux for your wedding?" Lia had learned that it was best to talk about what was on her mind, rather than to hold it in when she was speaking with Antonio. It was the only way they were really going to get to know one another again.

"Yes, it was. And I'm okay wearing it, if that's what you're wondering." He always seemed anxious to put her mind at rest, and Lia did love that quality about him.

"We've not really talked about that relationship. About why it ended?"

"Is it important?"

She could tell by his tone of voice that to him, it didn't feel important for her to know.

"Well, ending an engagement seems like a pretty big deal. Was it you or her that called it off?"

"It was me."

She didn't know if this was a better or worse answer. Down the trail of questions she continued.

"Why did you call it off? Did you decide that you didn't love her?"

Antonio looked thoughtful as he waited a few seconds to respond. "No, it wasn't that exactly. We were in love." He squeezed Lia's hand. "And now that love is only a memory. I've since made way for someone new. For you, my darling."

Lia breathed a sigh of relief that they were able to have these serious conversations without its being too uncomfortable. But they had a long way to go yet.

"So why did you end it, then?"

"Well, I felt that Bianca—my ex—had changed. I had

the realization that my life was becoming something that didn't really feel like me any more. In the beginning, she was happy when it was the two of us together, doing simple things. Then her career started taking off and her father gave me a position at the company that he owned. All of a sudden my days consisted of wearing a suit and tie, going to fancy lunches and big events in Roma most evenings. I started to really hate how pretentious everything felt."

Lia couldn't put her finger on exactly why, but his words were making her feel uneasy. Maybe taking him to the opera and making him wear a tux was going to be a mistake. But she felt it was about Arianna and a way for him to know his daughter better through the things that only Lia could tell him—share with him.

She nodded to Antonio. "Yes, it is hard for me to imagine you dressing in a suit and tie every day." She smiled broadly. "Although I bet you look very handsome dressed up."

"Well, hopefully you enjoy looking at your man just as much in my jeans, t-shirts, and work boots." Antonio winked.

"Are you my man?" Lia laughed lightly, feeling her face grow hot.

"I sure do want to be."

Lia looked down at the pasta that Sofia had just placed on the table for them and then back up at Antonio. "I'm pretty sure I'd like that—for you to be my man. And yes, I very much enjoy looking at you in whatever attire you have on."

They were both silent for a moment, and Lia guessed that the same thought was going through Antonio's head as her own. *Or whatever you don't have on.* She tried to push the image aside as they focused on their lunch, and the conversation turned to less serious topics. There would be time. They needed to be patient with one another and their relationship. She felt the importance of not rushing things no matter what her heart—or body—told her. She'd waited this long for something that she never even thought was possible. She could let their relationship develop naturally. At least she hoped that she wouldn't do anything to mess it up.

PAULA KAY

CHAPTER 24

The air was cool as Antonio drove the car with the windows down through the Tuscan countryside. Lia laid her head back against the seat as she watched him drive, admiring his profile. He had a strong nose and chin that any Italian man would be proud of. His hair was as thick as she remembered it when they were younger, with only a hint of gray beginning to show at his temples. She thought the gray made him look all the more handsome.

Antonio glanced over at her as he pulled up to a stop sign, reaching out to grab her hand and flash her a grin. "What are you thinking about?" he asked, bringing her hand up to his lips to give it a quick kiss.

Lia smiled back at him, feeling completely content in the moment, continuing to remind herself to try to relax and enjoy the drive—and the entire weekend—with Antonio. They hadn't discussed it specifically, but she felt that this weekend was going to say a lot about their relationship and where it was headed. She had spent so much time worrying about it—thinking that Antonio was going to change his mind, remembering his earlier anger at her for all of the things that she'd kept from him over the years. She wouldn't blame him, really. But he had assured her over and over again that he did forgive her, that she had to let it go if they were truly going to have a chance at making something work between them.

She felt Antonio tugging on her hand playfully as he continued driving along the road to Florence.

"So you don't want to share with me what you're thinking about?" He glanced at her and winked.

Lia laughed. "Sorry. I guess I was distracted."

"By...?"

"By you." She tapped him lightly on his thigh, trying not to notice his muscles through the perfect fit of his jeans.

"Me?" The tone of his voice teased her with the insinuation that maybe he wanted to know exactly what she was thinking.

"Yes, you. You look so handsome." She felt her face growing warm, a sure sign of the red creeping onto her cheeks as it seemed to do so often these days around Antonio. She wondered if she would ever feel completely comfortable around him and not quite so overwhelmed.

"Well, if you think I look handsome then it's a perfect compliment to your beauty. You look so beautiful today. In fact, I can't wait to stop this car and take you in my arms." He teased her with his hand moving to caress her bare leg just above her knee under the skirt she wore.

She reached down to place her hand over his, just in

case he had the intention of moving farther up her leg, but enjoying his touch nonetheless. She breathed deeply, allowing herself to feel the pleasure that just the simple touch from him brought to her. And he didn't go further, but looked just as intense as she felt.

"You do drive me crazy, you know."

His voice was a bit husky, and at once Lia imagined him whispering it in her ear. They really needed to either pull off the road or stop this nonsense immediately. She wasn't at all sure if either of them could handle it for much longer. As if reading her mind, Antonio moved his hand back to the outside of her skirt, patting her leg gently as he did so.

"Bella."

She knew what he meant without more words. And they continued on for the remainder of the drive mostly in comfortable silence, Lia lost in romantic thoughts of the weekend to come and guessing that Antonio was having some thoughts of his own that, hopefully, he would share with her later.

They arrived at the Four Seasons, and Lia was surprised at the shock of emotion she felt as they headed towards the front desk to check in. Watching Antonio look around at the magnificent lobby, she was instantly reminded of being there with Arianna and her own wonder at being in such a place. Tears stung her eyes as she thought about the irony of being here now with

Antonio while feeling the rush of emotion that always threatened to overtake her with memories of her—of *their* daughter.

"What do you think?" She smiled at him as they stood at the front desk waiting for their room keys.

"I think it's beautiful."

The funny look on his face as he responded did not go unnoticed by Lia.

"But?"

"But nothing. It's beautiful. And so are you." He reached over to brush her lips with a quick kiss.

"You're going to love it here. I promise."

At least she hoped that he would love it as much as she had. She caught him glancing at the well-dressed couples coming and going throughout the lobby and wondered if he felt out of place in his jeans and white t-shirt. She certainly wasn't bothered by it, although she couldn't wait to see him in his tux the next night; and she was pretty sure that he had packed appropriate clothing for the restaurants that they'd be dining in. If she was being honest with herself, she hadn't felt at all comfortable when she first arrived with Arianna, either. Her daughter had been living a lavish lifestyle that was so foreign to Lia. But she had been so generous with her and tried to make Lia feel so comfortable that she'd quickly forgotten the financial divide that made such a big difference between them.

And now here she was trying to embrace that part of

Arianna's life once again. She wanted that for Antonio
too. She could give him things if he wasn't too proud to
accept them. And how Arianna would have loved that.
To know that part of what she'd left for Lia was being
shared with her father. Lia felt sure of this. She'd have to
tread carefully, though, because she did know Italian men
to be very proud and stubborn when it came to accepting
gifts and being able to provide for their families. She had
learned that from her father and suspected that Antonio
was not different when it came to such things.

She reached over to grab Antonio's hand as they
followed the bellhop to their suites, which were right next
to one another.

As Lia sat in the restaurant later that evening across
the table from Antonio, she was flooded with memories
of Arianna once again. She'd had the foresight to not
attempt to book either of the same suites that she and her
daughter had stayed in. That would have been too
strange. But she did have a good cry in her room earlier
when she and Antonio had parted ways to get dressed for
dinner. She'd really had no idea how intense she'd be
feeling, and wondered now if coming here had been a
mistake.

"Lia? Bella?"

Antonio was trying to get her attention.

"What? Sorry." She laughed lightly, reminding herself
how special this night was meant to be. "What were you

saying?"

"I was just wondering what you were thinking. You looked so deep in thought." He took her hand across the table. "And I was wondering which wine you would prefer tonight?"

"Sorry. Yes, I have been having a lot of memories of Ari, I must admit." She looked down for a moment before she continued, her voice a whisper. "It is hard— being here. Harder than I thought it would be." She squeezed his hand when she noticed the pained look on his face. "But I'm glad to be here with you now. I didn't mean that I wished I wasn't."

"I know. It's okay. I do want you to tell me all about the last time you were here with—with our daughter. Let's get some wine, shall we? Would you like the white?"

"No, I'll have the Chianti." Lia said quickly.

"Really? I thought you preferred white wines." He seemed to be studying her carefully, and she couldn't help but wonder what he was thinking.

"No. Well, I used to, yes. But ever since I met Ari, I've grown to really like the Chianti. It—it reminds me of her."

"Bella, I think everything reminds you of her." He said it quietly, and she couldn't tell exactly what it was that she detected in his voice.

"And do you think that's bad?" She felt herself growing a bit defensive and tried to not show it as she waited for Antonio to answer her. "Well? Do you think it's bad that I want to remember our daughter?" She pulled her hand away.

Antonio reached for her hand again, giving it a squeeze. "No, bella. I don't think it's bad to remember her. But I do think that most of the time, the memories don't seem to make you very happy. If I can be honest?"

Lia nodded for him to continue, wondering if she really wanted to hear what he had to say next.

"It seems to me that you are pretty set on keeping her memory alive in a way that serves your grief—your depression about losing her."

Lia pulled her hand away again, instantly feeling the tears spring to her eyes. This was *not* starting out well at all.

"Darling. I don't mean to make it sound as though there is anything wrong with grieving—with missing Arianna. It's just that sometimes it feels that you are trying so hard to stay in the grief of it all. But instead, maybe remembering her should be about thoughts that make you happy for the time that you had with her. The things that you want to share with me about her—about our daughter."

She felt him trying harder.

"I'm sorry. I shouldn't have said that. The last thing I want is to ruin the evening with you. I do want you to tell me about her, and I know that you have many memories of being here with her; so let's just leave it at that, okay?" He got up to come around the table, bending down to give her a kiss on the lips. "The last thing I want is to hurt you. Can we just forget that I said any of that?"

Lia kissed him back and nodded in reply, but she felt a wall going up between them. The rest of the dinner felt awkward. The food was as delicious as she remembered it, and Antonio seemed to be enjoying his steak, but the conversation was strained and she felt that he was as anxious to retire to his room as she was to hers. She didn't have any thoughts about them sharing the same bed that night, and she suspected it was the last thing on his mind too.

CHAPTER 25

Lia awoke the next day after a fitful sleep. This weekend had started out the way that she'd hoped, and she was determined to turn things around between her and Antonio today. They'd planned for coffee in her suite that morning, so she spent the next hour having a bath and getting ready for their day together. He'd agreed to let Lia plan the entire weekend, which she had done, but now she was second-guessing everything that she had lined up.

There would be the dinner and the opera that night—even though she knew it was risky, given the conversation that they'd had last night, she was determined that it was something that they needed to do together. Something that Arianna would have wanted, and that was more important to her than anything else. That much she did know. She wouldn't compromise on the promise that she'd made when she felt the shift occur weeks ago. When she decided to really give her life in Italy a try and to always keep her daughter's wishes for her in mind. She desperately wanted to honor the memory of her, and this was the best way that she knew how.

She'd originally planned to go to the market for some shopping and lunch and then head over to walk the steps of the Duomo, to be able to enjoy the beautiful views from the top. But now she wasn't at all sure if it was a good plan for the day, because each thing that she'd planned was something that she had shared with Arianna. Given the thoughts that Antonio had shared with her over dinner last night, she wasn't sure that she wouldn't end up being an emotional mess. It seemed risky, and the whole point of the weekend away was for her and Antonio to draw closer together.

Lia's thoughts were interrupted by a knock on her door. She took a deep breath and smoothed her hair before opening it to the welcome sight of Antonio, who quickly grabbed her in an embrace.

"Good morning, beautiful. How did you sleep?"

She instantly felt relief. "Very well, thank you. And you?"

"Good. The bed, the suite, everything is so comfortable." He eyed her carefully before taking her hand to lead her to the sofa in the sitting area. "I'm really sorry about dinner last night—about what I said. I feel very bad about that, and I can't even begin to imagine everything that you must have gone through—are still going through. Can you forgive me?"

He looked so forlorn that all of Lia's doubts and

worries about where they were at with their relationship vanished.

"Of course, and there's no need to be sorry. Really. They may have actually been words that I needed to hear. And—" she reached over to give him a hug. "And I know that it is I who should be begging you for forgiveness. I went through a lot losing Ari, yes. But I took so much away from you. I can't begin to understand the pain of how that must feel to you."

"Shh." Antonio pressed his lips against hers in what seemed like an effort to stop her apologies. "I've told you that I've forgiven you and I meant it. I only want to move on from it. That's all. Yes, it's still painful at times, but I want to know about her. So yes, I do want you to share the memories that you have with her. But, the thing is—I want to know about you too. Does that make sense?"

She nodded, but inside she felt very confused. If she was being honest, she'd not felt like herself for a very long time. Certainly not in the year since Arianna's death. It was hard to remember who she had been before she'd met her daughter. And she wasn't so sure that she liked that person very much. *But did Antonio like this person that she was now?* She was beginning to have her doubts and she wasn't quite sure what to do with them. Room service arrived, and so she brushed the thought aside as she took the coffee offered to her. She just needed to focus on Antonio today, and she was sure that things could get back to normal for them. Just in time for the nice evening she had planned.

Lia and Antonio had climbed the steps to the top of the Duomo. After discussing her plans with him and knowing that they had a big evening ahead, they opted to go straight to the Duomo for the morning, foregoing her idea of heading to the market first. The climb had been nice, with easy conversations and stolen kisses at various viewpoints. The morning was feeling easier and like they were more themselves.

Antonio reached out to tuck a strand of hair behind her ear as they stood in the light breeze looking out over the famous view: the Arno River wound through the city with the many small bridges scattered along its length. Lia was quiet as her thoughts took her back to the day that she'd been here with her daughter.

Antonio came up behind her, sliding his arms around her waist, encouraging her to lean her slight frame back into the strength of his chest. She breathed deeply, trying just to let herself enjoy the moment.

"What are you thinking about? Are you okay, bella?"

"Yes, I'm okay." She turned around to convince him of her words with a kiss. "I'm more than okay." Smiling, she looked at him. "Isn't it beautiful up here?"

"*Sì*, yes, it is. I've been here before but it was many years ago. I can see why it is such a popular spot."

"Yes, Florence is so pretty. Do you miss living in the city? In Rome?" She thought about how strange it had been picturing him there while she was shopping with Rebecca.

"No, I don't miss it at all. I wasn't meant to be a city guy. Having the vineyard now has confirmed me of that. Not being outside in the fresh air and sunshine was very stifling to me. I hated having to go to the office every day, putting on a suit and tie." He looked at her, pulling her close again. "What about you? Do you see yourself settling now in Castellina?"

Lia thought for a moment. "Yes. I mean, I don't see myself anywhere else in Italy. If I moved at all, I suppose it would be back to San Francisco, where I have my friends. But I do like it here and I'm enjoying the restaurant a lot, hard work and all."

"You were meant to own that restaurant, bella." Antonio smiled. "I didn't forget how much you used to talk about it when you were younger. Or all of the times that you spent cooking in your mother's or my mother's kitchens."

She smiled at his reference to the many memories that she herself had as well. "I can't help but to think how wonderful it would have been if both of our parents could have seen us together now."

"Well, I'm not so sure if your father would have approved." Antonio laughed. "That was rough going in the beginning."

"That's only because he caught his daughter sneaking off to meet some strange boy working in the fields." Lia's laughter joined his. "Once I was honest about our relationship and introduced you, he liked you. And so did Mama."

"I was worthy of his little girl, then?"

He turned her face towards his for a kiss, and Lia found herself lost in the moment kissing him, both of them oblivious to the many tourists who had made their way to the top of the steps.

"You were always more than worthy." She kissed him quickly before grabbing his hand to pull him towards the stairs. "I say let's make our way down before it gets any more crowded. And I think I could go for some food. How about you?"

"Do you know what would make me insanely happy right now?" Antonio said.

"What's that?"

"Well, I can think of a few things, but since we're still out in public, I'd say a nice little pizzeria somewhere quiet with a bottle of wine—and my favorite girl sitting across from me." He patted her playfully on the behind and winked at her when she turned around, grabbing at his hand.

"Oh, so I'm your girl now, am I?"

"I think you've always been my girl, Lia." He stopped and pulled her to him as he stepped to the lookout at the side of the stairs. "I mean that. I've never stopped thinking of you. I think a part of me always wondered."

She loved the serious look on his face. The way that

he was so open with his feelings for her. It scared her and made her feel excited at the same time. Her heart leapt in her chest as she pressed her lips up to his in a deep kiss that she hoped expressed everything that she was feeling for him in that moment.

"Me too." She tilted her head back to look him in the eye. "I never stopped thinking about you either. Even when I thought you were married, although I hate to admit that. I would never have tried to contact you, but I couldn't get you out of my mind, try as I would."

He grabbed her hand again as they finished their descent down the steps and out onto the square below. "Well, I for one am excited to see where we are going to go from here. You know I've been a little skeptical when it comes to relationships ever since my break-up, but with you, I'm really trying. I don't want to waste any time. I'm trying to just trust what I'm feeling, and so far being with you feels very good to me.

"Me too."

She let him lead her down a quiet street to a pizzeria that someone had pointed out to them, and they spent the next few hours enjoying a huge pizza and the nice bottle of white wine that Antonio chose for them.

PAULA KAY

CHAPTER 26

Lia glanced over at Antonio sitting beside her, so handsome in his tux. She was still so shocked at times when she looked at him, wondering how it could be that she'd been given a second chance. They were seated in one of the best box seats at the opera house in Florence and *La Bohème* was about ready to start. Antonio reached over to kiss her quickly on the cheek and whispered in her ear.

"You look *so* gorgeous in that red dress, bella. I don't think I will be able to take my eyes off you all night."

She smiled back, feeling her face grow hot at the compliment, and wondering if tonight would be the night that they'd take their relationship to the next level. She kissed him back, lingering a bit longer on his lips. "You look every bit as handsome as I'd imagined you would," she whispered back. "And this is so lovely, isn't it?"

She wanted him to agree with her but she got the sense that he wasn't at all sure how he felt about being there. She had second-guessed her choice for a moment when they'd had the discussion about his ex and what had gone wrong in their relationship. On the one hand, she knew that he probably wasn't going to be entirely happy going to the opera, but on the other hand she felt duty-bound to Arianna to show this—part of what had been her world, the things that she'd loved to her father. *Surely he would want that too?* She didn't have time to have a discussion with him at the moment because the curtains were rising, signifying the start of the performance. They had a long night planned, so she knew she'd have a chance to talk to him more later; and if all went well, she hoped that she wouldn't be sleeping alone.

She sat back to watch the performance, and to her shock, found herself drifting off at times. She'd quickly glance over to Antonio to see if he'd noticed, and saw his eyes closed a few times as well. If she wasn't feeling so mortified, she'd laugh out loud at the situation. Neither of them must have slept after their big morning walk, and it was showing in their energy level now. Apparently *La Boheme* was not enough to keep them occupied and prevent their drifting off to sleep.

Lia sat up straight in her chair, nudging Antonio awake with her leg. He reached over to take her hand, smiling as he mouthed the word "sorry" to her. She winked back, trying to make light of it but noticing the change in her own mood. Something was wrong if they couldn't, for a few hours, just enjoy a single performance. What was wrong with them? Surely he didn't hate it that much. But she saw his expression out of the corner of her eye and knew that he was bored out of his mind. She'd definitely planned the night badly, and hoped it could be salvaged.

Seated in the dining room back at the hotel for a late glass of wine after the opera, Lia noticed that Antonio was looking uncomfortable in his tux and couldn't contain his yawns. She tried to laugh it off, but their conversation had turned a little strained after the performance. Now she was trying her best to salvage what was left of the night, knowing that it would probably be ending soon—and not quite the way that she'd hoped, by the looks of things.

Lia raised her glass in a toast. "To a nice night at the opera."

Antonio clinked her glass half-heartedly; he looked like he was holding something back.

"What is it? Did you really find the opera that boring?" She tried to use a teasing tone but it was coming out all wrong. She could tell it from his face the moment that the words left her mouth.

"Well, did you like it?" He looked at her pointedly as if daring her to say otherwise. "I saw you drifting to sleep too, you know." He laughed and she was happy to hear the teasing at least.

"I wasn't really sleeping." She looked him in the eye. "Well, okay. I was tired, I admit. That walk up the stairs wore me out this morning, I guess. But back to you. Did you not enjoy it at all?"

Antonio studied her face for a few moments before he spoke quietly. "Not really, Lia. I mean, I appreciate the effort that you went through to book it—the special box seat and everything—especially your beautiful gown."

She saw his eyes move to the plunging neckline of her dress.

"Now that, especially, I appreciate very much." He grinned and she couldn't help but laugh. "I just don't know. I mean, it's not really my thing. Does that bother you?"

She didn't answer him right away as she thought about the question for a few seconds. It wasn't that it really bothered her so much as that she felt very confused about her old way of life and her new way of facing the world—with her new wealth, with everything that Arianna had given her, and trying to live up to that expectation of what her daughter would have wanted. She and Arianna had shared such great times together when they were in Italy and everything had been new to Lia. The drivers, the fancy dinners, hotels, the opera, the clothes. Arianna had opened Lia's eyes to a whole new way of life, and she somehow felt that she owed it to her daughter to share that kind of lifestyle with the father that she hadn't had the chance to know. She looked at Antonio now, who was patiently waiting for an answer.

"Does it bother me that you didn't enjoy the opera? No, not really."

"But?"

She knew that her comment had insinuated a 'but' coming directly after.

"It's just that I'd like you to try some new things. The things that I did learn to enjoy with Ari."

Antonio looked very uncomfortable, and for the first time since the day that she'd told him about their daughter, she thought she saw anger flash across his face.

"Lia, this isn't really anything new to me. I told you that. This *was* the lifestyle I was living in Rome—with Bianca. And it didn't work for me. It's not that I have a problem taking you to a nice meal or a performance once in awhile if that's something that's important to you. I can do that. But if you're looking for me to subscribe to some type of lifestyle that has me back wearing fancy clothes and having to be at some nice restaurant at a certain time most nights of the week, I'd be lying to you now if I said that I'd sign up for that again."

Lia couldn't stop the tears from stinging her eyes, and she wasn't even entirely sure why she was crying.

"Darling, please." Antonio reached for her hand and she could feel his tension easing a bit. "I do adore you. And I guess I'm not saying that anything is off the table. I'm not. I just find it all a bit confusing, because from where I'm sitting, you look very beautiful and are saying all the right things, but I'm not entirely sure that this is all what you want either."

She felt his eyes probing hers, wanting some truth to

come out of the conversation.

"I liked the opera just fine. I did. And this, the fancy clothes and restaurants is all new to me, Antonio. I've never had any of it before. I never really even wanted any of it." She was aware that her voice was growing louder and she couldn't contain the growing frustration about the conversation and the whole evening here with Antonio, which had gone nothing like she'd planned.

"I know that, bella." He looked like he was about to say more. "I think we should probably just call it a night. We're both tired, and we have a long day ahead of us tomorrow if you still want to do a few things here before we make the drive back."

Antonio reached for Lia's hand as he stood up from the table, and Lia felt that her heart was breaking just a little bit at the way the evening had turned out. She couldn't really blame him, though. They had talked a bit about lifestyles and he'd made some valid points, including the questioning of her own feeling about the way she was trying to live her life these days. She felt a real unsettling of emotions within her and knew that sleep probably was the best thing that she could do for herself. For both of them. They'd probably feel more up to talking in the morning; she'd just have to save her ideas for a romantic night together for another time. A night that she hoped would come anyways.

CHAPTER 27

Lia poured another glass of wine for herself and Rebecca, who'd come into the restaurant to have lunch with her and hear all about the weekend away with Antonio. Lia was still feeling a little stressed about the whole thing, if she was being honest with herself, and she'd hoped that maybe her friend could shed a little positive light on the whole situation. Things hadn't quite been the same between her and Antonio ever since they'd returned home a few days earlier.

"So tell me everything," Rebecca said, sipping her wine and looking at Lia with a teasing smile of expectation.

"Well, honestly, there's not much to tell, I'm afraid."

"What do you mean? Was it not a good weekend?" Rebecca said.

Lia felt herself tensing up a bit at the memory of it. "Well, no. It wasn't the weekend that I'd hoped for. That's for sure."

"What happened?" Rebecca asked. "Did he not like the opera?"

"Oh, he definitely didn't appreciate the opera. He practically slept through most of it."

"Oh?" Rebecca raised an eyebrow.

"Well, honestly, I nodded off a few times myself, which made it all the more strange when we were talking about it afterwards." Lia laughed lightly at the memory of noticing herself falling asleep in the fancy box seat.

"Okay, well, that sounds kind of funny, actually. And hard to believe that it would ruin your whole weekend. Did you at least—"

Lia cut her off. "Nope. We didn't share a room or a bed. There was way too much friction between us in the evenings, or we were too tired. Or I don't know. I honestly am not sure that *he's* ready to take it to that level."

"That surprises me. He's so affectionate with you all the time."

"He is, yes. And I love that about him." Lia smiled as she spoke. "I think it has a lot to do with his break-up. And also the fact that we have this past together and well—quite frankly, the secrets that I've kept from him."

"I think he'll come around." Rebecca said.

"He's said that he has forgiven me—that he just wants to move forward with our relationship. And I do believe him. I just think it must be hard, you know?"

Rebecca nodded her head in agreement as Lia continued.

"I think he definitely does have some walls up, and I

don't blame him. And really, things just felt a little off all weekend. It was actually pretty horrible. We'd have our moments and then a little setback, like the night of the opera. I found myself feeling very frustrated and I think it was the same for him." Lia sighed, not wanting to bore her friend with the details. "So that's where things stand. But enough about me. How are things with you and Marco?"

"Oh, Marco and I are fine and sickeningly in love." Rebecca laughed as she got up from the table, coming around to give her friend a quick hug. "Speaking of Marco, I have to run because I promised him that I would attempt cooking for him tonight."

Lia got up to hug her friend goodbye. "Oh, that sounds great. Remember my offer always stands whenever you are ready to come try a few things with me in the kitchen. I'm very happy to do that, and I'm sure Carlo would be too."

"Thank you. I'm sure I will be taking you up on that offer at some point. For now I'm just focusing on boiling water for the pasta I purchased at the local shop."

"Travesty," Lia teased.

"And I'm sure that things will be back to normal with you and Antonio soon. Try to hang in there with him. I have a very good feeling about you two."

"Do you?" Lia laughed. "That's just because you are living in one fairy-tale love story right now."

"Maybe so. But I do think things will work out." She

turned to wink as she opened the door to leave the restaurant.

No sooner had Lia sat back down to finish her wine than her phone was ringing with a call from Antonio. They had only texted since arriving back from Florence a few days earlier; Lia knew that he was also very busy getting caught up at the vineyard, so she'd tried to push thoughts of him not wanting to see her out of her head. Nonetheless, she felt very happy to see his name showing up on her caller ID.

"Hi, Antonio."

"Darling, how are you? I'm so happy that you answered." She could hear the genuine delight in his voice and instantly felt more at ease. She loved that he was so expressive with his emotions. She thought it was rare for many Italian men, and felt pretty lucky that Antonio had somehow learned something in his past that allowed him to be so forthcoming. She didn't particularly remember him being that way when they were young, although he had been very romantic even back then.

"I'm okay, thank you. How are you?"

"Just okay?" He paused to wait for her reply.

'Well, certainly I wish that things would have gone a little better between us towards the end of the weekend, you know? I feel really bad about that. And yes, if I'm being honest, I'm very happy to be talking to you now," Lia said.

"Well, I feel bad too, bella. Actually that is part of why I'm calling you. Can we spend the afternoon together? Tomorrow? This time I am planning the date."

She could hear the teasing in his voice, which caused her to smile on her end of the line.

"Yes, I can get off work tomorrow. What did you have in mind?"

"It's a surprise. Nothing fancy. *At all.* Just dress comfortably and I will come by the restaurant at two o'clock to pick you up, okay?"

"That sounds great. I'll look forward do it."

"*Ciao*, bella."

"*Ciao.*" Lia clicked off the phone, feeling much better then she'd felt since leaving Florence. Maybe things were going to get back on track with her and Antonio after all.

PAULA KAY

CHAPTER 28

Lia let Antonio lead her out of the restaurant, delighted at how he had been teasing her about their date. Their reunion after even just a few days had made her feel missed and special. He'd grabbed her in a big hug just as soon as he'd seen her, and she realized how much she had missed him.

"So where are you taking me? And why all the mystery?"

"No real mystery. Just something I've been wanting to do with you. It's not far. We can walk from here, actually. I hope that you are in the mood for something sweet, bella."

They walked in silence holding hands, and it wasn't long before Lia realized exactly where he was taking her. Walking to the little cafe where they'd shared their last gelato together as teen-agers, she felt a rush of memory. He stopped along the lane, pushing her gently against the stone exterior of a corner of one of the buildings. Hidden from passersby, he surprised her with a passionate kiss.

"Do you remember, bella?" he whispered against her

lips.

She nodded her head, unable to speak as the memory flooded over her and her lips met his in another passionate kiss. God, they really were like a couple of teenagers, kissing and groping one another as if everything about it were new and exciting. She laughed.

"What's so funny, my darling?"

"Just being here with you like this. Having you kiss me the way that you do. I feel like a kid again." She smiled as he pulled her tighter.

"Ah, then my secret plan is working." His face grew more serious then. "I hated letting you go that day, saying goodbye to you, not knowing when I would see you again."

"It was the same for me too, Antonio. It was." She desperately wanted him to believe her.

They continued on along the lane until they came to the gelato shop.

"Shall we?" Antonio asked.

"I love something sweet in the afternoon."

"Do you?" He was teasing her again, and she got the message behind the simple question.

They ordered their scoops of gelato to go, and continued walking to the square and the exact bench where they'd said their goodbyes so many years ago. They sat in easy silence for several minutes, each lost in their own thoughts, Antonio's hand resting lightly just above her knee.

"Antonio?"

"Yes?"

"Can I ask you something?"

"*Si*, you can ask me anything." He leaned over to give her a quick kiss on the cheek.

"Why didn't you write me back? After those first few months, I mean?"

Antonio looked at her and waited for a few moments before replying. "It will always be one of the deepest regrets of my life, bella. Especially knowing what I know now. That maybe things could have been different. Things would have been different had I known you were pregnant." He looked at her carefully, as if checking her emotional state.

She was surprisingly keeping it together somehow, even though it was a topic that nearly always filled her with regrets. In some ways it felt comforting now hearing Antonio talk about his own regrets. It was the closest that she'd felt they were meeting on a common ground, not that she wanted him to feel half the pain that she'd been feeling all this time.

She answered, "I know. I wish that I'd been more careful about making my decisions back then. I wish I would have trusted you—trusted in us. I just was so confused when all of the communication stopped. I didn't know what to think except for imagining that you'd moved on without me—that you'd found someone else."

"I know. You had every right to think that. And the

truth is that that's exactly what had happened. Well, not that I'd fallen in love or anything. There was no one that could take your place, even back then. I just didn't know how to move on without you. I remember feeling lonely, and all of my friends were talking about how you were sure to be meeting lots of men in America." He pressed gently on her leg as if willing her to understand the depth of the teenage heartbreak that he was referring to.

"I was so stupid, Lia. Really, all of the secrets that you'd kept from me were just as much my fault. I know how difficult that time must have been for you. It really kills me that you went through all of that alone."

Lia couldn't help the tears from coming now, and she saw them in Antonio's eyes as well as he pulled her head to his chest. She felt so safe with him in this moment, the past becoming a distant memory of hurts and regrets. And she almost felt confident that they'd be able to overcome it, if they did it together.

Antonio lifted her chin off his chest slightly as he looked in her eyes. He traced the contour of her face, tucking a few strands of hair behind her ear, and reaching down to gently kiss away the tears that had fallen to her cheeks.

"Do you know what I do know, bella?"

She looked up at him. "What's that?"

"I like being here like this with you now. Even though what we're talking about is difficult, it feels real. Like we're making some steps forward."

"Yes, I agree. I like it too." And she thought about how different it felt being here with him now as compared to how the past weekend had felt—and she got it. What he had meant by everything said during their weekend in Florence. They felt more comfortable together here in this place because it was more similar to how they'd been when they first met and fell in love. She felt more like herself just now than she had for a very long time.

CHAPTER 29

Lia was racing around her house putting the last things in place before her guests would arrive. There were fresh flowers in all the bedrooms, chilled wine in the fridge, and a special little dollhouse that she'd gotten for Jemma to play with. She was looking over her list one more time, certain that she'd been forgetting something, when she saw the limousine pulling up the long driveway. She'd hired the car to pick them all up at the airport in Florence.

She saw Jemma out the window first as the child darted out of the car for the front door.

"Look who it is," Lia said, smiling, as she opened the door to receive a giant hug from the young girl.

"Hi, Lia," Jemma said, her eyes darting around the house behind her. "Mom says that I can go for a swim in your pool."

"Jemma." Blu mouthed the words "driving me crazy" to Lia behind Jemma's back. "Jemma, be polite and say hello. And you need to ask Lia if it's okay to use the pool."

Jemma looked at Lia, who nodded.

"You just need to be sure that there's a grown-up out there with you, okay? Come here and give me another hug."

Jemma obeyed and Lia bent down to meet her eyes. "How was your flight? You seem to have a lot of energy, so I assume that you slept."

"I did. And yes, it was very good. I'm going to go put my swimsuit on now, okay?"

"Okay; let me say hello to your mom and then I will show you your bedroom."

"It's okay, I can find it." Jemma scampered off, leaving Blu and Lia looking at one another.

Blu reached over to give Lia a big hug. "That child is driving me nuts." She laughed; Gigi nodded her head coming in the door with Douglas right behind her.

"She is getting to be a bit of a handful." Gigi smiled at Lia and gave her a kiss on each cheek. "It's so lovely here, Lia."

Lia smiled back and showed Douglas where to set down the two suitcases that he was holding. "How have you two been? Did you enjoy your time down south?"

"*Sì*, yes. It's been so wonderful to spend time with my sisters. I think Douglas has gotten quite used to all of the magnificent Italian cooking." Gigi laughed as Douglas comically rubbed his tummy as if to signify the weight he'd put on. "I only hope he won't be spoiled when we return home and it's back to take-out five nights a week."

Douglas laughed as he kissed Gigi on the cheek. "Darling, you've been trying. That's all one can ask for." He turned to Lia. "And don't worry. I've saved lots of room for more fabulous meals that I know are coming our way here."

Lia laughed at the sudden little swirl of activity around her. It already felt so good to have her friends here, in her home. She'd been planning this time and the party at the restaurant for some time now, and wanted every detail to be perfect.

"Well, come in. Let me give you a tour of the house; and then how about if we take some wine outside by the pool so Jemma can try it out?"

"That sounds lovely. And I had no idea that your place would be so big." Lia caught the quick look that Gigi had shot Douglas. "It feels nearly as big as the place that Ari—the place where we stayed the last time we were all here together. I hope you are not renting this one just because of our coming?"

Lia had told them that she hadn't had to purchase just yet, and Douglas had expressed his willingness to help her if there was any negotiating to be done. "Oh, well, no. That's not the only reason, although I do admit that I love having plenty of room here for you guys."

"Well, because this might be a tad big for just you, yes?" Gigi said.

Lia felt herself growing irritated by her friend's questioning. It was a reminder of the conversation that they'd had only weeks before when Lia was still living at the guest house. She'd finally made the move out of it, and now she couldn't help but feel slightly judged by her choices.

"No, it's really not too big. Besides, I'm not making any decisions just yet anyways."

"I know you're not. I'm sorry. And I should talk. Putzing around the big house in Sausalito feels very weird to me so I'm probably projecting my own feelings onto you."

"No worries," Lia said as she gave her friend a quick hug. "I'm just glad that you've all arrived and we can enjoy the space together.

Lia finished showing them their rooms and the rest of the villa before leaving them outside on the patio with a very excited Jemma, who was ready to jump straight into the pool. "Have a seat and I'll be right out with some wine."

Lia busied herself in the kitchen with the wine and a tray of meats and cheeses that she had prepared ahead of time. Just as she was about to step back outside she overheard a hushed conversation taking place between Gigi and Blu.

"—feels kinda weird. Almost exactly like the time we were all here with Ari," Blu was saying to Gigi. "I mean it's so lovely, but I really hope that she is finally doing some things for herself."

"*Si*, me too. We will see how she's doing soon

enough. What we can't do is overwhelm her with questions," Gigi was saying to Blu.

"Speaking of questions…has she said anything more to you about Antonio?"

"No, I know that they were going away for a weekend but we never talked after that."

Lia couldn't see their faces but imagined a look being shared between the two women.

"I just wish that she would relax about it a little bit. You know, let things happen naturally. I'm afraid that Antonio might get overwhelmed with it all," Blu said.

"It's a lot to take in. The important thing is that she's being honest with him. That she did tell him about Ari," Gigi said.

"You two hush now," Lia heard Douglas saying when it sounded like he was just getting back to the table. "Let's not give her a hard time. She's been through a lot of changes, this big house being one of them. Let's enjoy our time here and not be sticking our noses into all of her business—"

"*That* sounds like a good idea to me." Lia set the tray down along with the bottle of wine, knocking it a little harder against the table than she had meant to. "Douglas, if you could get the glasses from the kitchen, I'll let you serve yourselves." She was aware of the cold tone to her voice, but it was all she could do to keep from bursting into tears. "I'm just going for a little walk. I'll be back."

Gigi got up to follow her. "Lia, don't go. Come talk to

us."

She could hear the slight panic in her friend's voice, and for a moment she thought about turning back. But she was angry. And she had a right to be. It wasn't fun to be thinking that your every move was being second-guessed by every person in your life. And she *had* come so far. Ever since Gigi had left here weeks ago, she'd made that promise to really try to give it her all, to keep Arianna's wishes in mind. And she *had* been doing that.

She had only walked for about ten minutes when she felt better, enough to go back and confront her friends. She wouldn't make everyone uncomfortable by not talking about the conversation that she'd overheard. That wouldn't make anything better. It was better to talk about it so that she could say her piece and then get on with it.

Blu came to meet her as soon as she could see her in a distance.

"I'm so sorry. That was stupid. We should have just waited and had a conversation with you. Lia?"

Lia looked at her and nodded.

"We just care about you. You know that, right?"

"I do, yes. But it sure doesn't feel good when you all seem to be questioning every decision that I'm making," Lia said.

"I know. You're right. And I'm the last one who should be criticizing anyone," Blu said, and Lia wondered what was behind the offhand statement.

She'd have to try to remember to have a good chat with Blu before their visit was over. They'd not talked for a long time, and despite her irritation with the young girl, she really did want to know how her clothing line and everything was going.

The two women walked back to where the others were sitting outside. Lia looked at everyone sitting around the table who had supported her over this past year. They really *had* become a little family of sorts to her, and she knew that they did have her best interest at heart. She was probably just feeling overly sensitive because of all the pressure she'd put herself under with their arrival and the party she'd been planning for them at the restaurant. She really wanted everything to be perfect, and doing do, she knew, was causing her a great deal of stress.

"Alright, everyone," Lia said as she walked up to the table. "I appreciate your concern and I love you all very much, but you're just going to have to trust that everything is okay. Deal?" She looked around the table at each of their faces.

They all nodded, looking solemn and sorry.

"I really want you all to have a great time while you are here, starting with this party I've got planned at the restaurant tomorrow night," Lia said. "I'm excited for you to meet Rebecca and Marco."

"And Antonio?" Gigi asked.

"Yes, I think he's planning to come too," Lia said. "And no grilling him." She laughed, trying to lighten the mood.

"I can't wait to see Sofia," Jemma said. The two had gotten along splendidly the last time Jemma was here, and Lia knew that Sofia would be pleased to see the young girl.

"She will be happy to see you too." Lia smiled at Jemma wrapped in her towel, wet hair dripping. "Now why don't you go get changed and we'll have a little walk before dinner."

Lia wanted to continue talking to the others and didn't think it was appropriate conversation for Jemma to overhear. She wanted to set them straight with everything she'd been thinking—make them understand that she'd meant it when she told Gigi a few weeks ago that she was finally digging herself out of the emotional pit that she'd been in since Arianna's passing. That she was finally ready to do the right thing by her daughter, living the life that Arianna had wanted for Lia.

And she needed to apologize for stomping off. Her friends' being there meant everything to her, and she hated that it had started off so badly.

CHAPTER 30

Lia and Carlo had closed the restaurant the day of the party. It had been hectic; with so much to be done in the kitchen, Lia found herself frazzled and running around at the last minute to pick up the added items to make the dinner just perfect for her guests.

Gigi and Douglas had arrived early to help her. Gigi was following her around in the kitchen and Douglas was hanging a few pictures in the restaurant that Lia had saved to put up just for the occasion. Lia was trying to be patient, but Gigi was talking her ear off about her stay in the south with her sisters last week and she found herself growing irritated with her friend.

"Sorry, Gigi. Can we talk about this later, please?" Lia said, recognizing the hurt expression on her friend's face. "I'm just so busy right now and quite frankly, I could use some help."

"Of course. I'm sorry. What would you like me to do?" Gigi's mouth was tight, and Lia instantly regretted her harsh tone.

She reached over to give her friend a hug while handing her an apron. "I'm sorry. I do want to hear all about your trip and your family. I'm just feeling a little bit stressed out at the moment. Can you stir the sauce on the stove, please?"

Gigi nodded and began stirring in silence.

She'd have to fix that later, spend some time with Gigi when everything was over.

Lia sighed and texted Sofia, concerned that she hadn't turned up yet with the beef from the butcher. Lia had placed a special order for the new recipe that she was making and she'd barely have time as it was. She continued to knead the dough for the pasta, and moments later Sofia entered the kitchen out of breath.

"Sorry, I got your text but was just on my way back. Lia, there was a mix-up and they didn't have your order today," Sofia said matter-of-factly.

"What?" Lia did not hide her irritation. How was this happening to her, today of all days?

"He apologized and said that he would have it for you tomorrow."

"I don't *need* it tomorrow," Lia said, her voice rising.

Carlo came up behind her. "It's okay. We can make something else. There's plenty of pasta here and I can whip up a couple of pizzas. Let me get the dough going."

Lia ran her fingers through her hair, suddenly feeling very tired. More tired than she'd felt since arriving in Italy a few short months ago. "I don't want to serve my guests

pizza, Carlo." Her voice was loud and she didn't try to
hide the irritation she was feeling.

She felt Jemma's arms around her waist from behind
at the same time as she heard her squeals of laughter from
being chased into the kitchen by one of the waitresses.

"Save me, Lia. She's gonna get me." Jemma laughed
behind Lia's back.

Lia pried the child's hands off her waist, turning
around quickly. "Jemma, get out of the kitchen. There's
not enough room to be running around in here." She
didn't realize how loud she had yelled until she saw the
little girl's face, tears welling in her eyes.

Lia bent down to give her a hug. "I'm sorry, Jemma. I
didn't mean to yell at you. I'm just trying to get the dinner
organized. Can you go play in the front room, please?"
She saw Blu entering the kitchen as Jemma nodded in
response, her eyes wide.

"What's going on in here?" Blu said, as Jemma passed
right by her without stopping. "Is she bothering you?"
she said to Lia.

"No. I did yell at her, though. And it wasn't her fault.
I'm just feeling a bit overwhelmed with everything." Lia
felt the tears stinging her eyes. "Sofia's just informed me
that we no longer have the beef for the menu, and I'm
not quite sure what I'm making now."

Gigi came up beside her, giving her a slight hug. "Let
Carlo make the pizzas. We'll have that with the pasta and
salad and it'll be great. Lia, get yourself a glass of wine, for

goodness' sake. You're getting way too worked up about nothing, really. We don't care what we eat. Isn't that right, Blu?"

Blu nodded her head in agreement. "We're just happy to be here with you."

Lia walked over to the small desk at the side of the kitchen and sat down in the chair; her shoulders slumped and the tears fell freely.

Crash!

Everyone jumped in the kitchen at the loud sound that they'd heard up front. Lia's heart pounded as she ran out to the front room, knowing before doing so what the sound had been. Douglas was standing amidst the pieces of the broken picture frame, looking completely forlorn as Lia caught his eye.

"I'm so sorry," Douglas said quickly as Lia bent down to pick up the large photograph that was sitting underneath the jagged glass. "I should have waited for someone to help me, I guess. I thought I could hang it myself and—well, it just slipped out of my hands."

Lia walked over closer to the wall, to a spot where the floor wasn't covered in glass, and slumped down holding the picture of Arianna in her hands. The tears were falling now and she didn't bother to acknowledge Rebecca, who was suddenly beside her with a glass of water and a box of tissues. She just sat still and let the sobs overtake her. The room was quiet, everyone seeming to realize what was necessary in the moment. Finally she took a deep breath.

"This is just all wrong." She looked around the room at her friends, noticing the absence of Antonio. "I wanted everything to be so perfect. For this to be a celebration to honor Ari—and all of you. I've been trying so hard and it's just—it's just not working. Nothing is working." Lia continued to sob and felt Gigi next to her, taking the picture of Arianna out of her hands.

"Lia, what *exactly* isn't working? What are you trying to do here?" Gigi wasn't one to hold back her thoughts, and she had something on her mind to say now. Lia knew that look and the tone of her voice well.

The others had seated themselves at various places nearby and Lia knew that everyone was waiting, some with looks of confusion on their faces at what was going on—at this little breakdown that Lia was apparently having.

"Gigi, you know how much I've been trying." Lia didn't bother to try to stop the tears from falling. She just felt so done. Out of the corner of her eye, she noticed that Antonio had slipped in and was watching her from across the room.

"With all of this." Lia swept her arm around the room in a quick motion. "Ever since that day that you and I talked about Ari and what she would have wanted for me. With Antonio, the restaurant, everything here. And I've been trying *so* hard to do all of this for her. To honor her memory. And nothing seems to be going right. I can't even have one simple party turn out well." She sobbed harder, knowing that her friend was about to respond.

"Lia, you've got it all wrong." Gigi waited for Lia to look up. "This girl——" She held up the picture of Arianna in front of Lia's face. "——your daughter." Gigi motioned for Antonio to come nearer. "She didn't want you to do anything *for* her. Don't you get that?"

Lia felt her sobs subsiding a bit as Antonio sat down next to her on the floor, taking her hand in his as they both waited for Gigi to continue.

"Here you are, living this life that you *think* Ari wanted you to live, but from what I can see, from what we all can see——" Gigi looked around the room at all of their friends as if to make a point of their solidarity behind her words. "You're just going through the motions of living a life that Ari might have lived—a big fancy home that you probably aren't totally comfortable in, expensive clothes, even this big party. And for the record, Ari would have loved a big pizza party with her closest friends."

"I was just trying—I don't know what I've been doing, really. I didn't know what to do with all the money—with all of this." Lia honestly felt confused but somewhere deep down she felt something shifting inside her as she looked to Gigi to continue.

"I know—we all know that you've been doing your best. And we get that it hasn't been easy for you. We do. It's just so obvious that this isn't working for you. And frankly, I can't bear to just stand by and watch it any longer."

"But what can I—I just don't understand what you—what Ari would have expected from me, I guess," Lia said, letting her head fall to the side a bit to rest on Antonio's shoulder.

No one spoke for several seconds, Lia appreciating the momentary silence as she worked to collect her jumbled thoughts.

"Stop me if I'm out of line with this or completely wrong—" Antonio looked to Gigi for the nod of her head before he continued. "I think what Gigi—what all of your friends are trying to say is that Arianna didn't want you to live some kind of idea of what you thought her perfect life would be. I'm guessing that your—that *our* daughter was trying to make your dreams come true when she left you all that she left you. She must have known how you felt about this restaurant and what it would mean for you to be able to come back here to live." He waited for Lia to respond to his words with a nod. "You've told me as much yourself."

"Yes," Lia said in a quiet voice, trying to fully let his words sink in.

"And honestly, Lia. I've felt so confused trying to get to know you these past weeks. There've been moments when we've been together where no time has passed at all. Like when I first saw you, and eating gelato on the bench in the old square. That was the girl that I had fallen in love with so many years ago—the woman that I'm falling in love with again now."

He brought Lia's hand to his lips, and she felt her heart beating at his words.

He continued. "Other times—like our weekend away in Florence, at the opera and, from what I'm guessing, this scene I walked into tonight—you don't seem like anyone I've known before. It seems like you're trying to be someone you're not, and it's been confusing to me."

Lia looked around the room, her instinct telling her that some of this conversation should be said in private, but at the same time feeling the significance of it in this room with all the people who loved her so much. "I'm sorry, Antonio. And to all of you. I really hadn't realized any of that, as crazy as I know it must sound. I've just been trying to find my way back to feeling somewhat normal, to not feeling so sad all of the time."

"We all understand that," Gigi said. "And no one wants anything less for you than your happiness. God, Arianna especially wanted that."

Lia and Antonio stood up, and Lia walked over to where Gigi stood to hug her friend, feeling Blu's arm come alongside her waist on her other side. "I do know that," Lia said. "That Ari wanted me to be happy."

"I know what Ari wanted for you." Blu spoke quietly at Lia's side. "She told me during that last week—before she died—that she knew the guilt and unhappiness that you'd been feeling. She knew the release of that same guilt for herself—how she felt when she finally forgave herself for giving up her own daughter. She was just like you when it came to that, you know."

Lia's eyes filled with tears again, remembering the intense conversations that she'd had with Arianna about what she'd felt about her own daughter and the pain of knowing that she would die before ever being able to tell her how much she loved her.

"Lia, Ari just wanted everything for you. Everything that she'd known that you'd given up when you made the choices that you made. That's why she left you this restaurant. That's why she thought that you'd be happiest back here in Italy. It wasn't at all about you having all of the money to create a life similar to hers. She was well aware of how different your tastes were, even though you tried so hard to accommodate hers since the moment you first met. She didn't care about that. She only cared that maybe she could make some of *your* dreams come true. She felt happiest thinking that finally it could be *your* time to have everything go well for you, to see your dreams fulfilled." Blu stopped to look at Antonio, standing there beside Lia, holding her hand and looking at her with pure love in his eyes.

"God, this—you two. If you had any idea how happy that would have made your daughter." Blu laughed as Lia and Antonio looked at one another.

"Well, I just don't quite know what to say." But Lia was smiling now as she spoke. "I'm just so thankful that you all are here, that you all have loved me through so much this past year." She gave Antonio's hand a squeeze as she continued. "I think that everything you've been saying to me is true, and I think that I've really not gotten it until now."

She took a deep breath as she looked around the room. "And I think I finally get it." She grinned broadly and felt the weight of the world lifting from her shoulders. There were a lot of changes to be made, and she was going to tackle them with a renewed sense of purpose—she glanced at Antonio by her side—and with this lovely man beside her.

"Carlo, about those pizzas?" Lia called into the kitchen and then laughed as she saw him already taking them out of the oven. She grabbed the hammer and a few nails that she saw lying on the counter, handing them to Douglas. "Can you just put up the picture of Ari over where we discussed, please? I'll get another frame for that later. Sofia, can you turn the music on please—the *La Boheme* track is fine—and I'll go get the Chianti."

She started for the kitchen, then turned back for a moment. "Everyone please have a seat. We're about to have a much-needed party in here."

CHAPTER 31

Lia jumped at the knock on her door.

"Come in."

"Hi. I hope I'm not disturbing you," Gigi said.

"No, not at all. I wanted to talk to you alone anyways—to apologize for how I spoke to you earlier today. Come, sit here by me." Lia patted the big space next to her on the king-size bed.

Gigi crossed the room to sit next to her friend. "It's okay. I know that you've been under a lot of pressure—we all know that."

"I'm so thankful for your support and that you're all here. It makes me miss you all so much, though." Lia smiled.

'Well, we sure do miss you too," Gigi said.

Lia reached over to give her friend a slight hug.

"I have something for you," Gigi said, handing her a large envelope.

Lia turned it over and looked at her friend, confused. "What is it?"

"Open it," Gigi said. "It's an essay that Ari had submitted to a publication before she died. It wasn't accepted so it was returned in the mail. It was in the forwarded mail that Douglas just received yesterday."

Lia opened the envelope and slid the single typed paper out on the bed in front of her, glancing at Gigi as she read the title, "I Hope She Knows".

Gigi leaned over to give Lia a quick kiss on the cheek. "I'll leave you alone to read it."

Lia smiled slightly, a bit shocked that she'd suddenly been given this unexpected gift from her daughter. She took a deep breath, flashing back to all that had happened and been said last night at the dinner. She fluffed up her big pillows behind her on the bed and settled in to read the words that her daughter had written.

I Hope She Knows
by Arianna Sinclair

When I was young, I thought my life was perfect. All of my friends said it was so, and their lives also seemed pretty perfect, so I believed them. My father worked hard for everything that we had, and I knew it was a certain kind of perfection that he was trying to achieve. I thought that he'd done that for us—with our fancy house, expensive cars, the vacations, and even the big allowance he'd been able to afford for me. It was all pretty perfect…until it wasn't.

The day everything started to unravel for me was not the day that my parents died, as one might think. That day was rough, for sure. And all of the trauma that followed after that wasn't easy. Even the day that I was told that I only had months to live was not the worst day of my life.

The worst day of my life was also the best day of my life. That was the day I met my birth mother.

When I first saw her, I instantly saw myself. Not just in the way she looked, but also the recognition of a lifetime of guilt and shame. A lifetime that would be so much shorter for me, which gave me all the more reasons to get it right. I loved that moment when our eyes first met. I hadn't yet broken down my walls against trust but instinctively knew that I wanted much more time than what we had. The realization of that was the worst I'd ever felt.

My mother helped me to have the happiest days of my life towards the end. And I'm sure that they ended up being some of the worst days of her life. The sorrow I've felt for that has threatened to overwhelm me at times, yet I push on, knowing there is little else to choose.

We've had this time together for reasons I'm sure that neither of us can fully comprehend. I hope she knows how happy knowing her has made me. I hope she knows that I loved her and forgave her ten times over in the end. I hope she can forgive herself for the mistakes of her past, that she will go on to live a happy life filled with love and contentment and every single thing that makes her smile.

I hope she will remember the times we had together with fondness and not tears. I hope that someday she'll find the love that I didn't have the chance to know with a man. I hope she'll remember that life can be short sometimes. That people come and people go.

I hope she'll know that I wanted her to be happy, and I hope *my mother knows how much I loved her.*

Lia put the paper aside as she took a deep breath, allowing the tears to come.

But there was something very different about these tears. She hoped that by some chance, Arianna was looking down on her now, seeing the effect that reading her words had had on her. Leave it to her daughter to continually give her so much more than anything she ever deserved.

Almost as soon as the thought was in her head, she pushed it aside. Enough with the negative talk. It was time to be done. If she'd learned anything from her daughter, it was that. *What was she waiting for?* Arianna was right. Life was fleeting, and spending another moment of it with guilt and overwhelming sadness was not honoring Arianna or herself.

She got it now. Everything that all her loved ones had been trying to tell her all this time. It had taken her awhile, but she was fully there. It was time to start living her life for her. To finally put aside the guilt. If Arianna had forgiven her, then it was time for her to forgive herself.

Lia got up to go find Gigi and the others, telling them how much what she'd read had effected her. It was time for moving on. She was ready, and they were there with open arms to support her just as they always had been.

CHAPTER 32

Lia stood in the doorway of the kitchen in her new villa surveying the group of friends sitting around the dining table of her new home, finishing off the meal that she'd prepared for them. It had been a small miracle that the home had still been available for purchase and for her to move into straightaway. Gigi, Douglas, and Blu had all extended their trips in order to help her move in; and even though it was more crowded than the bigger villas in the area, Lia had insisted that her friends fill up the guest rooms.

She walked back into the kitchen, turning her attention to the dessert she had brought out from the refrigerator. She felt Antonio's hands around her waist, heard him sniffing the scent of his favorite perfume on her neck.

"Bella, I see you've turned into my little rocker chef in here," he said in reference to her favorite music playing in the background while she cooked. "I like it." He nuzzled her neck with a kiss.

Lia leaned her head back onto his strong chest. "I like it too."

She smiled, thinking about how far she'd come. Standing here in the kitchen with Antonio now really felt like coming full circle. Finally she'd learned how to truly let go, how to be guided by Arianna's wishes and the wealth that her daughter had left her, without getting lost in a life that wasn't hers to live.

She took Antonio by the hand, guiding him quietly through the door into the small living room with the fireplace that she loved.

"I have one last thing to unpack that I wanted to show you." She walked over to the box on the floor, picking up two framed pictures, placing them gently on the mantel. Antonio came over beside her, taking her hand in his as he looked at the pictures.

"She was so beautiful," he said, picking up the framed shot of Arianna that Lia had captured when they were at the market in Florence. Her dark hair was a mass of tangles in the light breeze, her smile wide as she posed for her mother that day. And right next to the picture was a shot of Lia and Antonio that they'd taken with her phone during their gelato date in the square. In it, the forgiveness of the past and the hope for a future had been captured so perfectly. They were two young lovers hurled through time and space yet brought together to begin anew.

Antonio walked over to the two glasses of Pinot

Grigio that he'd poured for them, handing one to Lia and raising the other in a toast. "To our daughter——" Lia clinked her glass to his as he continued. "——for bringing you——my love, back to me."

Lia felt tears stinging her eyes, but for the first time in a long time, they were tears of sheer happiness. Antonio pulled her to him as the sounds of laughter from the other room filled the silence of the moment.

"*Ti amo*, my darling."

"I love you too, Antonio."

ABOUT THE AUTHOR

Paula Kay spent her childhood in a small town alongside the Mississippi River in Wisconsin. (Go Packers!) As a child, she used to climb the bluffs and stare out across the mighty river—dreaming of far away lands and adventures.

Today, by some great miracle (and a lot of determination) she is able to travel, write and live in multiple locations, always grateful for the opportunity to meet new people and experience new cultures.

She enjoys Christian music, long chats with friends, reading (and writing) books that make her cry and just a tad too much reality TV.

Paula loves to hear from her readers and can be contacted via her website where you can also download a complimentary book of short stories.

PaulaKayBooks.com

ALL TITLES BY PAULA KAY

http://Amazon.com/author/paulakay

The Complete Legacy Series

Buying Time
In Her Own Time
Matter of Time
Taking Time
Just in Time
All in Good Time

Visit the author website at PaulaKayBooks.com to get on the notification list for new releases and special offers—and to also receive the complimentary download of "The Bridge: A Collection of Short Stories."